FADE TO BLACK

"There are no evidences of violence or of suicidal intent. All symptoms listed are entirely compatible with the theory of *death by misadventure*. So you see, Miss Withers—"

"Stafford was about two thirds swacked and he fell off a chair and busted his neck," Chief Sansom put in heavily.

"I'm telling you this, Miss Withers, because we want you to be perfectly satisfied," Mr. Lothian of Mammoth Studios continued. "And I might point out to you that in the forty-some years since the motion-picture industry moved to California there has been no major crime committed inside the walls of any studio!"

"There's a first time for everything," said Miss Withers. "Of course, I had a talk with Stafford before he died and he told me he was afraid of being murdered..."

"A coincidence," Lothian told her. "If he wasn't pulling your leg. The man had a mania for playing jokes, you know."

"But death had the last laugh," she said, and made her exit.

Bantam Books offers the finest in classic and modern American murder mysteries. Ask your bookseller for the books you have missed.

Stuart Palmer

THE PUZZLE OF THE SILVER PERSIAN
THE PUZZLE OF THE HAPPY HOOLIGAN

Craig Rice

MY KINGDOM FOR A HEARSE
THE LUCKY STIFF

Rex Stout

AND FOUR TO GO
BAD FOR BUSINESS
THE BROKEN VASE
CURTAINS FOR THREE
DEATH OF A DUDE
DEATH TIMES THREE
DOUBLE FOR DEATH
A FAMILY AFFAIR
THE FATHER HUNT
FER-DE-LANCE
THE FINAL DEDUCTION
GAMBIT
THE LEAGUE OF FRIGHTENED MEN
MURDER BY THE BOOK
PLOT IT YOURSELF
PRISONER'S BASE
THE RED BOX
THE RUBBER BAND
SOME BURIED CAESAR
THREE DOORS TO DEATH
THREE FOR THE CHAIR
THREE MEN OUT
THREE WITNESSES
TOO MANY CLIENTS

Victoria Silver

DEATH OF A HARVARD FRESHMAN
DEATH OF A RADCLIFFE ROOMMATE

Max Byrd

CALIFORNIA THRILLER
FINDERS WEEPERS
FLY AWAY, JILL

R.D. Brown

HAZZARD

Sue Grafton

"B" IS FOR BURGLAR

Robert Goldsborough

MURDER IN E MINOR

Ross MacDonald

BLUE CITY
THE BLUE HAMMER
GOODBYE LOOK
THE MOVING TARGET
SLEEPING BEAUTY

A.E. Maxwell

JUST ANOTHER DAY IN PARADISE

Rob Kantner

THE BACK-DOOR MAN

Joseph Telushkin

THE UNORTHODOX MURDER OF RABBI WAHL

Ted Wood

LIVE BAIT

Barbara Paul

KILL FEE
THE RENEWABLE VIRGIN

THE PUZZLE
OF THE
HAPPY HOOLIGAN

Stuart Palmer

BANTAM BOOKS

TORONTO • NEW YORK • LONDON • SYDNEY • AUCKLAND

*This low-priced Bantam Book
has been completely reset in a type face
designed for easy reading, and was printed
from new plates. It contains the complete
text of the original hard-cover edition.*
NOT ONE WORD HAS BEEN OMITTED.

THE PUZZLE OF THE HAPPY HOOLIGAN

*A Bantam Book / published by arrangement with
the author's estate*

PRINTING HISTORY
First published in 1941.
Bantam edition / November 1986

ISBN 0-553-26024-3

Published simultaneously in the United States and Canada

Bantam Books are published by Bantam Books, Inc. Its trademark, consisting of the words "Bantam Books" and the por-
trayal of a rooster, is Registered in U.S. Patent and Trademark
Office and in other countries. Marca Registrada. Bantam
Books, Inc., 666 Fifth Avenue, New York, New York 10103.

PRINTED IN THE UNITED STATES OF AMERICA

KR   0 9 8 7 6 5 4 3 2 1

Contents

THE PUZZLE
OF THE
HAPPY HOOLIGAN

1

I met a Californian who would
Talk California—a state
So blessed, he said, in climate
NONE HAD EVER DIED THERE
A NATURAL DEATH....

ROBERT FROST

He was on fire. Flames licked around him, and the building was about to collapse, and he couldn't jump from the window because the water from the firemen's hoses kept pushing him back into the room. That was the dream.

Consciousness returned so slowly to Wilfred Josef that there was a split instant of relief when he remembered all about being here at the Firsk's for cocktails. He even remembered making his getaway when the party waxed noisy (Josef liked only the noises he himself made when he set classics from his collection of limericks to music via the guitar) and his coming out to a deck chair on the moonlit patio for forty winks.

The sound of his own screams brought him wide awake. He found—like the young girl from Peru who woke up one night in a hell of a fright—that it was perfectly true. Or at least a big wad of crumpled Sunday newspaper was blazing merrily under his chair, and two laughing madmen were dancing withershins around him, yelling "Fire! Fire!" and squirting him unmercifully with soda-water siphons.

The other guests, carrying ping-pong paddles, half-finished drinks or bridge hands came rushing out through the doorway. But by that time Wilfred Josef (author of year before last's best-selling novel *Anastasia's Lovers*) was singed, sodden and impotent on a charred island in a lake of fizz water.

Mona Firsk, trying to make a noise like a hostess, rushed toward him, her stubby, ring-covered fingers outstretched in sympathy. But even for her the picture presented by Josef's amazed, naked face was too much. She was swept away in the rising tide of laughter, for he had lost eyebrows, lashes, and even most of the silky Vandyke which had been his pride and joy. He was mad as a wet hen and getting madder every second in spite of the helpful brushing off, the support into the house and the stimulants which were being offered as first aid.

Under cover of the hilarity two men faded quietly around the corner of the house, keeping in the soft dirt of the tulip beds. As they passed the swimming pool they paused there to cast adrift the seltzer bottles and then went on down the long flight of steps to the street and the line of parked cars.

There they stopped laughing and listened. "What are we listening for, Saul?" The speaker was Virgil Dobie, a vast, gargantuan man with pointed, Satanic eyebrows and the innocent eyes of a child.

Saul Stafford, a small, untidy man with a leonine head and a perpetually blue jaw, swayed slightly on his bandy legs. "We are waiting to see if some fool turned in an alarm." He seemed to feel the need of justification. "What else can you do with a man who wears a *zits* like that? And who insists on reciting limericks when you're trying to make a small slam vulnerable?"

Dobie nodded judicially. "In itself a grave social error.

But perhaps all this will be a lesson to him. Say, Saul, what are we listening for?"

Then they both heard it, far off. And coming closer.

Stafford turned toward the crimson Packard with the cut-down Darrin body. "I dislike open cars and I dislike your driving," he announced. "But drive me home anyway."

They rolled on down the driveway and were turning out of Bel Air's gray-stone gates when the fire trucks went screaming and careening past them.

Those same sirens, homeward bound a few minutes later, shattered the silence of the evening on Hollywood Boulevard, sounding even to the heights of a little room on the top floor of the Roosevelt. Miss Hildegarde Withers sat up in bed, her hair in curlers and a wry smile upon her long, equine visage. Sirens in the night and the rumble of trucks—it made her suddenly homesick for Manhattan. "This is a fine way to start a vacation," she scolded herself sternly, and plumped the pillow.

In the beginning, like any other middle-aged school-teacher with a savings account and six months' sabbatical vacation, Miss Withers had planned the usual Mediterranean cruise. And then Europe exploded, making it seem the better part of valor to see America first.

So here she was in Hollywood to her own mild surprise. With an itinerary all planned, including side trips to the San Fernando Mission and the La Brea tar pits in Hancock Park.

And to the Brown Derby on Vine Street where noon next day found her doing justice to an excellent omelet *aux fines herbes*. As is the custom of tourists in that justly celebrated restaurant, she was amusing herself by trying to match up the caricatures on the walls with their proto-types among the great and near great of Never-Never Land.

At which point trouble in the shape of a strange, excited young man in a bright plaid suit came over and plumped down beside her. "You," he accused, "are the 'Murder Lady.' Want a job?"

"I beg your pardon?" In spite of herself Miss Withers' expression of shocked propriety changed to a quick alertness.

"My name's Wagman, Harry Wagman," he went on, taking it for granted that she would recognize the name. "Picked you out from your picture in this afternoon's *Herald-Express*."

Here he displayed the paper, and Miss Withers looked dubiously at a reproduction of a too-candid shot of herself in the act of shaking hands with Chief of Police Amos Britt of Avalon, Catalina Island. The heading began, "SOUTH-LAND WELCOMES SLEUTH—Miss Withers Revisits Scene of Triumph."*

She nodded. "What was that you said about a *job?*" During her several adventures as an amateur criminologist the maiden schoolteacher could hardly remember a single time when her services had been requested by anyone. Indeed, it was usually in spite of hell and high water that her insatiable curiosity had managed to get her into a case.

"Right! This job would pay you *that* a week, maybe more." Wagman wrote the figure "$300" on the tablecloth.

Now she knew that there was a catch to it. "You don't solve murder mysteries by the week," she told him. "Besides, I haven't read anything recently about a local murder."

Wagman was amused. "Ever hear of the Borden case back in Rhode Island or somewhere?"

"What?" Miss Withers peered at him very suspiciously. "That happened nearly fifty years ago. And in the opinion of most experts it was quite thoroughly solved."

"Please! Just a minute, lady. This job wouldn't be for you to solve the Borden case." Wagman stopped, bit his lip and then wrote a name on the tablecloth. "*Thorwald L. Nincom*. Ever hear of him?"

"The movie director?" she said uncertainly.

Wagman winced. "The *producer*. Mr. Nincom makes

---

*See *The Puzzle of the Pepper Tree*, Crime Club, 1933.

the biggest superepics in Hollywood. Well, listen. It isn't officially given out yet, but he's going to do a picture based on the Borden case, a big super-A picture, in technicolor. And I'm going to sell you to Nincom!"

Miss Withers gulped, and her eyebrows went up. "That sounds very cozy, but——"

"Leave it to me!" insisted Wagman. "I'm your agent and for a measly ten per cent I take care of everything." He wrote the percentage down on the tablecloth. "You'll be technical adviser on the picture, see? Mr Nincom always has technical advisers on his pictures. Last year when he made *The Road to Buenos Aires* I got Madame Lee Francis a three months' contract. And what she can do you can do!"

The schoolteacher hesitated and was lost. So far she had been in town three days and had not once passed through the portals of a moving-picture studio. When she got back to Jefferson School the other teachers were sure to ask, "Ah, did you once see Gable plain, and did he stop and speak to you?" or words to that effect. It would not be nice to confess that she had drawn a blank. On the other hand . . .

Mr Wagman, taking her consent for granted, was already talking into a telephone which a waiter had mysteriously plugged into the side of the booth. An appointment was arranged for noon tomorrow at Mammoth Studios and made official by Wagman's writing place and hour down upon the linen.

As the schoolteacher passed out of the restaurant she could not help looking up at the wall and picking out a spot where one of these days her own likeness might hang. Then a soberer idea presented itself. All that she knew about the Borden case was the silly jingle beginning, "Lizzie Borden took the ax and gave her mother forty whacks. . . ."

Noon tomorrow finally became noon today, and Miss Hildegarde Withers rode up to the main gate of Mammoth

Studios in a bright yellow taxicab after a trip which took her well over most of southern California by way of Robin Hood's barn. The size of the tariff shocked her almost speechless.

"Listen, lady," the driver told her, "there ain't but two picture studios actually *in* Hollywood. That's R.K.O. and Paramount. The rest are scattered all over the map. And if you think Mammoth is a long haul try Metro or Warners'. They're twenty miles apart."

"When in Rome..." quoted Miss Withers to herself, and tipped the man a munificent quarter. "I'm going Hollywood already," she decided.

Harry Wagman stood in the Moorish gateway looking at his watch. "Now I'll do the talking," he told her. "It's as good as settled though. Did you see your publicity in this morning's *Reporter?*"

He showed the schoolteacher what appeared to be a small tabloid newspaper full of testimonial advertising and devoted to news of the industry. Halfway down a gossip column she read: "Plans for the new Thorwald L. Nincom production move apace.... Today he will sign a famous New York detective as technical expert on the picture."

"I haven't the slightest idea how that got out," said Wagman unblushingly. "But it can't do any harm. Here in Hollywood people don't believe anything, even their own love affairs, until they read it in print." And he steered Miss Withers inside the sacred gates. She had a brief glimpse of a reception room full of uncomfortable chairs and uncomfortable people, then of a double door guarded by a beefy young man in the uniform and badge of a policeman. The door clicked, and they went down a hallway and then outside into a street between towering, windowless buildings.

Young men on bicycles went lazily past them, bearing envelopes, sacks of mail, and round tin cans which Wagman said contained film, the precious strips of celluloid which were the sole product of this vast plant. Trucks rumbled by, and here and there were little groups of worried, older men in bright ties and sedate sack suits. There was no sign anywhere of a star or even of an extra player, but Miss Withers was oddly thrilled all the same.

Then they turned into a doorway and came at last into a spacious outer office hung with still photographs from old Nincom pictures, the likenesses of gigantic apes clinging to the Empire State Building, of stampeding buffalo and hooded knights of the Klan and of a lovely young woman tied very tightly to a railroad track in front of an oncoming train. All these assorted characters were enlarged to truly terrifying proportions.

This room was presided over by a lovely blond automaton with soft amber eyes and long magenta fingernails, whom Miss Withers took to be a movie star and who turned out to be Mr Nincom's third secretary. Wagman addressed her as "Jill."

Jill announced them to the Presence and for her pains received an angry masculine roaring. "I'm sorry——" she began. "But——" The roaring went on.

Jill's lip was a bit redder than normal when she turned to them again. "I'm sorry," she said coolly. "But Mr Nincom cannot be disturbed now. He's in a story conference with the writers."

Wagman nodded. "My clients also," he whispered proudly to Miss Withers. Then to Jill: "How're the boys coming with the script? Have they got it licked yet?"

She raised her eyebrows. "You mean Dobie and Stafford? Those two bums—I mean, they aren't working on the script at the moment. They got the ax."

Wagman wailed, "The devil! Why doesn't somebody tell me these things?"

Jill put through a phone call, turned back to them. "Don't ask me, Harry Wagman. They're your writers, not mine. And you can have them."

Miss Withers, a quiet bystander in all this, saw Wagman wink. To Jill he said, "Why, Miss Madison, are you and the boys still feuding?"

"I'm not amused at their punk gags, and neither is

the boss." She lowered her voice. "You know, *he* always likes to have his writers have lunch with him so he can be sure they don't take too much time out? Well, Dobie and Stafford decided they were tired of that and sick of the commissary food, so they brought lunch pails full of garlic sandwiches and *breathed* themselves right out of an assignment."

"They're under contract," Wagman observed cheerily. "Say, how about trying His Nibs again?"

Jill Madison tried again. Once more she was met by that crackling roar of words. She looked up, biting her lip. "I'm afraid you'll have to make another appointment," she told them.

Wagman shrugged and took Miss Withers' arm. "We might as well blow," he said dispiritedly. They went back again, out into the sunshine of the studio street. "I must say——" began the miffed schoolteacher, and then stopped short. Coming down the sidewalk was a penguin who wore a white sun topee, a blue sweater with the numeral "4" on its back and a polo mallet tucked rakishly under its flipper. Following, was a sunburned young man in the uniform of a ship's captain. He was talking to the bird, not too happily.

"Hi, skipper!" Wagman cried. "How's Pete today?"

The captain stopped and shook his head. "Not so hot," he admitted. "We were all set for a part in Zanuck's new picture where Pete was going to eat a bowl of goldfish, and then they decided to save money and hire two college boys from U.C.L.A. instead."

"That's Hollywood," sympathized Wagman. The captain started off again, and Penguin Pete, who had been patiently resting on his round stomach, rose and hurried after him.

"You never know in this town——" began Wagman. Then he stopped, looked back to where Jill Madison, her face flushed, was running after them.

"I'm sorry," she cried. "Mr Nincom didn't want you to go. If you'll come back and wait until the story conference is over he'll try to see you."

So they came back inside. Miss Withers sat down on a hard leather lounge beside the man who was to take 10 per cent of her salary if she ever got one and tried to avoid the accusing eye of the giant ape on the opposite wall.

It was a little more than half an hour before the inner door opened and a little procession emerged. Foremost was a slight youth with cropped hair and a hunted expression who was gnawing at the place where his fingernails used to be. "That's Frankie Firsk," whispered Wagman. "Son of Rupert Firsk, the matinee idol of the silents. Now the old man is retired and down to his last yacht, and Frankie is trying writing." Behind Firsk came a fluttery old lady who looked like the stage version of a London "char" and who was shaking her head and muttering to herself. "Melicent Manning—she wrote the scenario for the first picture Pickford ever did back in two hundred B.C." Then there was a wasp-waisted Slav in a green suit with an American flag in the buttonhole, and bringing up the rear was a stocky chap who looked like a middleweight fighter gone prosperous. His fists were clenched tight now, and he seemed to weave slightly as if he had run into a punch.

Wagman said, "Willy Abend, the pink playwright. And the last one is Doug August, the cowboy poet."

"All of them on one story?"

"There were two more yesterday," the agent advised her. "And there may be six more tomorrow." He rose and led her toward the desk again where Jill Madison was signing for a brown envelope delivered by a tall and dreamy youth. "Shush, Buster!" she was saying.

He was staring after the writers. "They get more a week than I get in a year," Buster went on. "And they're just a bunch of poops. Mr Nincom and his poops! Say, that's not bad, huh?"

"Not good," Jill said. She clicked at the switchboard.

"Lunch today? Just this once?" He beamed hopefully.

"No, thank you," she returned. To Wagman: "Just a moment, I think I can get you in. . . ."

Buster lingered. "'Girl who always buy own lunch

wind up old maid,' so Confucius say." Then he wandered away, his broad young shoulders sagging a trifle.

"Those fresh messenger boys!" Jill Madison observed.

"There is something in what he said, all the same," observed Miss Hildegarde Withers thoughtfully. "About buying your own lunch. *I* know."

Then the switchboard signal flashed three times, and Jill Madison nodded. The way was clear.

They were suddenly inside the paneled study of Mr Thorwald L. Nincom. Miss Withers stopped and blinked. Behind the largest mahogany desk she had ever seen was hunched a tallish man whose once good looks had run all to chins and paunch. He wore a green knitted shawl over his shoulders and with the fingers of one hand he constantly caressed the hairless dome of his head or tugged at his wispy mustache.

Mr Nincom acknowledged their arrival by holding up his pale hand imperatively and went on talking into the telephone.

"No, no, no—no—no! I saw those tests, I tell you. And Sheridan won't do for Lizzie. Listen, Artie, I don't want oomph; I want sizzle! *What?* Now, seriously, can you imagine the De Havilland girl killing her parents with a hatchet? It's got to be somebody else. *Of course*, Davis, only Harry Warner wouldn't ask any more than a pound of flesh for her. All right. Yes."

He hung up wearily, reached into his desk drawer and sniffed at a small bottle filled with bits of cork and aromatic spirits of ammonia. "The people I have to work with!" he moaned. "It was different when we were making silents. Ah, those days!" He suddenly frowned on his visitors, and Miss Withers wondered if she were expected to genuflect. But the great man turned to Wagman. "A type," he said judicially. "Most definitely a type! Might fit into the dead-pan, sour-puss New England background. But has she worked for me before? I always try to cast people who've worked for me before."

"This isn't for talent, Mr Nincom," Wagman hastily

explained. "I suggested that Miss Withers here might work out on the technical end—remember?"

"Hmm, possibly." Nincom waved them to chairs. "I suppose she's had experience along such lines?"

Miss Withers somewhat resented being spoken of as if she were not in the room. "I must confess, Mr Nincom, that I——"

She stopped talking because nobody was listening. "In this story," Nincom went on, "we are faced with bringing to the screen the epic biography of a fiery, inhibited woman—a daughter of icy New England. A great dramatic true story packed with suspense and murder and love interest, laid in the Gay Nineties with bicycles built for two, hoop skirts and bustles, everybody dancing the polka—it's bound to be powerful!"

Miss Withers saw that Wagman was nodding, so she nodded too.

Mr Nincom rose to his feet, produced a conductor's baton from behind his desk and started to stalk up and down, now and then pausing to conduct an imaginary orchestra. "A lovely young woman, driven to murder by a combination of circumstances. Or was she? After the jury sets her free, what then? What of the loyal sweetheart who has saved her from the noose? With the dark cloud hanging over her head, still hanging in spite of the acquittal, what can she do but send him away? Nothing!"

Mr Wagman shook his head, and Miss Withers seconded it. She was conscious of the fact that, half concealed by a screen in one corner, a small mouse-like woman was hammering a noiseless typewriter. And Mr Nincom went on and on.

The interview went swimmingly, as monologues usually do. At one time the schoolteacher had a sudden fear that she was being hired under the impression that she was Lizzie Borden herself, or at least a contemporary. With this point cleared up, and the newspaper clipping read aloud again by her agent to qualify her as a technical expert, all was serene. She listened as she was bound out

to Mammoth Pictures as a technical adviser on Nincom
production number 11–23 at a salary of five hundred dollars
a week with a four-week guarantee. "Your job is to make
sure that we follow the actual practice of the time, particularly in the detective stuff," Nincom advised her. "And,
please, I beg of you, keep this assignment absolutely to
yourself. Tell nobody the nature of your work. I don't want
Selznick to rush in and make a murder picture. The first
sequence of the script will be on your desk sometime this
afternoon, Miss Withers."

"My—my desk?"

Nincom pressed one of the many buttons before him.
There was a pause, evidently a longer pause than he
expected. He rang again, then snatched up one of his
telephones.

"Jill? What the goddam and all to hell——?" He
stopped. "What? Oh. Well, find her and tell her to get in
here and get in quick. Don't I ever get any loyalty and
co-operation around this place? What? WHAT?" He jig-
gled the instrument angrily.

Then, surprisingly, the door was flung open, and Jill
Madison entered. She was still the perfect secretary, still
the beautiful blond automaton, except that a loop of her
yellow hair had fallen rakishly over one eye and she
seemed out of breath.

"Yes, Mr Nincom?" she said in a somewhat choked
tone.

The great man relaxed, assuming an instantaneous
mantle of good fellowship. "This is Miss Withers, Jill. She
is joining our little family. Will you be good enough . . . ?"

His voice died away in his throat, for it was only too
apparent that she was not listening. Moreover, she was
making a noise.

It was a noise usually considered vulgar. Jill Madison
made it, not in the Bronx fashion, nor yet in the soft
Italian style, but with curled thumb and forefinger pressed
against her tightened lips, as they do within the sound of
London's Bow bells. When it had died away she bowed

and departed, slamming the door after her as a sort of punctuation mark.

For as long as one might have counted one hundred by tens all was dead silence within the sanctum sanctorum of Mr Thorwald L. Nincom. He did not look like a man amazed. He did not look angry. He simply stared at the door, as jarred as if a canary bird had spat in his eye.

Miss Hildegarde Withers had an uncomfortable feeling that all clocks in the world had stopped, that time was standing still. She cleared her throat. "You were saying...?"

That broke the spell. Nincom took a deep, shuddering breath and fumbled into the drawer for his smelling salts. "Have her report... Writers' Building," he managed to say, and waved them off.

In the outer office, by way of effective contrast, all was excitement. There was a little knot of men and girls around Jill, all noisily congratulating her. Harry Wagman loudly demanded, "What makes?" several times, but they were too busy to answer him. "Probably getting married and leaving the business," he told Miss Withers. They went on outside.

They were halfway down the narrow canyon of glittering white sunlight when there came the patter of footsteps behind them, and a small mouselike woman rushed up, thrust typewritten sheets into their hands. She turned out to be Miss Smythe, Nincom's number-two secretary.

"Here—I most forgot," she gushed. "Isn't it wonderful about Jill Madison drawing the favorite in the Irish Sweep? And maybe going to win a hundred and fifty thousand dollars?" She swallowed and rushed away again.

"Well!" observed Harry Wagman. "No wonder she blew her top." He looked vaguely around as if searching for a tablecloth to write the figures down upon. "A hundred and a half grand *isn't hay!*"

"What isn't which?" Things were happening a bit too fast for Miss Hildegarde Withers, and when Wagman deposited her at the doorway of the high, boxlike Writers' Building she was still dizzy.

"Just go right up to the third floor and tell the girl at the information desk that you're the new Nincom writer, and Gertrude will assign you to an office," he said. "I'll run over to the Administration Building and make sure this is all official. Good luck!"

"Wait! What's all this?" Miss Withers was looking at the typewritten sheets in her hand.

"Oh, that! You'll get used to it. I meant to warn you about Nincom's having a stenographer in his office to take everything right down on the typewriter for a permanent record of all conferences." He waved and departed.

The schoolteacher stood there, still staring at the strange and disconcerting record of her own uncertain speeches, at the rich, round phrases of Mr Thorwald L. Nincom interrupting her. She realized that she was getting into very deep water indeed, a world as different to her as a valley in the bottom of the sea might have been. It was a world in which to move cautiously.

She took a deep breath and climbed into the little automatic elevator which bore her waveringly upward. On the third floor she emerged to face a glass window marked "Information" with a small office and a large sultry-looking girl behind it.

"Sorry, but there is no soliciting in the building!" was the greeting.

"I beg your pardon?" The Withers eyebrows went up.

"Oh, aren't you with the Community Chest?"

Miss Withers explained that she would like an office. The sultry girl surveyed her long purple fingernails dubiously. "I don't know about that," she said. "Gertrude usually takes care of that and she's out to lunch. I'm Lillian Gissing from the secretarial department. I don't——Excuse me." A light flamed red on the board, and she pressed a key. "Third floor, Writers'. Who? I'm sorry, Mr Josef is working at home today. Yes." She turned back to Miss Withers confidentially. "The lies I have to tell! If I really said where he was—wow!"

"Really? But about my office?"

Lillian tapped purple fingernails against her rather prominent front teeth. "There's 303—Mr Dinwiddie has it but he's on his layoff. He won't be back for six weeks. . . ." She looked at the schoolteacher, making it plain that she did not think she'd last that long. "I'll stick you in 303." She slid a key under the window. "Next to the last door on the right."

It was a nice office. Miss Withers made up her mind to that the very instant she walked in. There was a big oak desk, a typewriter on a stand, two chairs and an uncertain-looking lounge. The one window was covered with a Venetian blind, but since the view consisted only of the flat roofs of studio sound stages, with some round brown hills beyond, that was small loss.

Connecting doors, both locked, opened right and left, and there was a radiator in the corner which she turned on at once.

The desk was bare and empty except for stationery, paper clips and some badly chewed pencils. Well, the powers that be were paying her ten dollars an hour to sit here, so she sat. After a while she took a sheet of letter paper from the desk and under the imposing letterhead she began typing a note to her old friend and sparring partner, Inspector Oscar Piper, back in Manhattan.

It began: "My dear Oscar, guess where I am! You wouldn't believe it if I told you! But Hollywood is the sort of place about which anything you can say, good or bad, is true. It is also a place where surprisingly novel things happen. . . ."

At that moment there was a click, and then the connecting door on her right opened suddenly. "Hey, Stinkie!" came a masculine voice.

Miss Withers blinked and looked up to see a short, blue-chinned man in the doorway, a man with a leonine head and wide, surprised eyes. He was holding a glass of water in a hand which trembled.

"Oh, I'm sorry," said Saul Stafford, backing away. "I

heard the typewriter and I thought old Dinwiddie was back."

"I'm afraid not," she confessed. "But since we're to be neighbors——" She introduced herself.

"Neighbors, eh?" He cocked his head, then spoke in a strange, excited voice. "This may sound funny to you, but would you mind tasting this water? To see if there's anything funny about it?"

She took the glass, sipped it. "It tastes like water to me. Why—you don't think it's poisoned, do you?" The remark was intended as a pleasantry, but when she saw his face she knew that it had rung the bell.

"Maybe," he said hoarsely. Then he shrugged. "Don't mind me. I've worked on so many quick B epics that I'm probably trying to live the part of Charlie Chan in the Death-Ray Tunnel or something. All the same, a lot of funny things have been happening to me lately."

"Such as?"

He shrugged. "Oh, near accidents to my car and funny-tasting drinks and so on. It's all a headache. By the way, you don't happen to have any aspirin kicking around, do you?"

Miss Withers was sorry. "Tell me more about these things that have been happening to you," she pressed.

But Stafford wisely shook his head. "There's probably nothing to it. I'm maybe a mild case of paranoia. But, anyway, I saw something in the *Reporter* just now—Nincom is importing a famous New York detective as technical expert on his new picture, and when the guy gets here I'm going to retain him and lay the whole thing in his lap!"

"But——" began Miss Withers, and stopped. She had given her word to Mr Nincom not to divulge the nature of her assignment.

"It's probably Ellis Parker," Stafford went on. "Or he's in jail, isn't he? So maybe it's William J. Burns or one of the Pinkertons."

He stood in the doorway nodding—a man supremely confident that he could see powerful assistance in the offing. Miss Withers followed, eager and unhappy. "I wonder——" she began, and stopped. For she was looking into Saul Stafford's office, into a room crowded with incredible objects, large and small. She noticed a typewriter stand equipped with an endless roll of paper, a high chair of the type used by tennis umpires, tables and desks covered with china animals, advertising statuettes, ship models, pipes and tobacco and every other imaginable object. The walls were covered with vast twenty-four sheets advertising the Folies Bergères, the Midland Railways and old Mammoth gangster pictures. One tremendous poster, an artist's conception of Josephine Baker wearing a G string, ran up one wall and halfway across the ceiling.

"No wonder," said the awed schoolteacher. "That room is enough to give anyone the jitters."

"We got started and we couldn't stop," Saul Stafford admitted. "It got so crowded in here that Virgil had to move across the hall, and still we keep collecting things." He shook his head. "Well, it's nice to have met you, Miss Withers. Drop in any time. I think I'll lie down and try to sleep off this headache."

With the connecting door closed again, Miss Withers returned to stare at the virgin expanse of her desk blotter. But she had no heart to continue her letter to the inspector. All she could think of was that frightened man next door who saw—rightly or not—the shadow of death all around him.

She had no idea of just how seriously Mr Nincom intended the pledge of secrecy to be taken, but he had been very pointed about it. It was a nice problem in ethics, complicated still further by the fact that Stafford would probably be very surprised to find that the famous New York detective he expected was really only the inquisitive spinster next door.

Should she tell him? Would he put any faith in her if she did tell him? Impulsively Miss Withers picked up the telephone and got through to Nincom's office where a bored young man answered and told her that the great man was out on the test stage. "Will you please ask him to call me the moment he is free?" she demanded, and the faraway voice promised to leave the message.

So she waited. There was something soothing and hypnotic in the air, but of course she couldn't go to sleep at the switch—not on her first day. She leaned back in the chair, staring at the opposite wall and a photograph of some tired-looking calla lilies, funeral lilies. She found herself slipping finally into a sort of waking dream in which that sheaf of lilies rested across the chest of Mr Thorwald L. Nincom. She, herself, a disembodied spirit, floated above the great man's funeral pyre, while around it, in a vast, wavering circle, danced his writers and secretaries and assistants, chanting a wordless, tuneless dirge.

The voices rose to a hideous cacophony. There was something she must do immediately, but she was bound in the dreadful paralysis of nightmare, bound and drowned and floating. Then she woke up suddenly to find that she was being shaken unmercifully by a tall and moderately frightened youth. It was Buster, the boy she had seen making calf's eyes at Mr Nincom's secretary. "Excuse me," he said, and slapped her face.

She tried to slap back, but her strength was gone. There was a sweetish-sick taste in her mouth, as if a stale lemon drop had died there.

"It's the gas," Buster was saying. "You have to light these heaters when you turn them on or else the room gradually fills up with natural gas. You all right, ma'am?"

"Of course I'm all right." She took deep breaths in front of the opened window, refused Buster's offer of a visit from the studio doctor, of a glass of water, of anything. "Though I'm very grateful to you, young man," she told him, "in spite of your rather drastic methods."

He grinned engagingly. "Confucious say, 'Better to wake up being slapped than sleep forever under tombstone.'"

Miss Withers frowned at him. "Sometimes I think

Confucious say too much. By the way, young man, do you mind a well-meant suggestion? The next time you want a blond young lady to go out to lunch with you why not forget about these synthetic Confucious sayings and quote something more powerful? Such as:

> *"Can such delights be in the streets*
> *And open fields, and we not see't?*
> *Come, we'll abroad, and let's obey*
> *The proclamation made for May. . . ."*

Buster looked at her, nodded. He said slowly, "I remember. . . .

> *"And sin no more, as we have done, by staying;*
> *But, my Corinna, come, let's go a-Maying."*

Yes, before I set out to learn the motion-picture business I was exposed to things like that. But I still think Confucious is more suitable to this town." He produced a large envelope, made Miss Withers sign for it. "From the Research Department," he explained, and hastened away.

Miss Withers shook her head. Hollywood, where messenger boys quoted Herrick and everything was topsy-turvy. She opened the envelope, found three books dealing with the Borden case. One was from the *Famous Trials* series, and she opened it at a paragraph discussing the theory that Lizzie Borden had stripped herself to the buff to save her blue calico dress before taking the ax to Ma and Pa.

She hastily turned a page. But after a moment she pushed the books away. Lizzie Borden was cold potatoes at the moment.

It was getting well on into the afternoon, and still no call from Mr Nincom. On a sudden impulse Miss Withers went over to the door leading into Stafford's office, knocked and tried to open it. The latch had been caught on the other side. That was odd. She knocked again. "Mr Stafford? It's I—Miss Withers."

Frowning, she went out into the hall and knocked on the main door to Stafford's office. Then she tried the knob and found that it turned. She went inside.

No, her neighbor had not gone home. The room was just as she had seen it before, except that now the gigantic poster of Josephine Baker hung from the ceiling by only one thumbtack, except that Saul Stafford himself lay sprawled akimbo upon the carpet.

There was a half-filled glass of water on the table beside a large bottle of aspirin tablets. The desk chair had been overturned, and three thumbtacks lay on the floor.

Stafford was beyond all help. She forced herself to make sure of that, felt the heavy leonine head roll loosely upon its broken neck, before she turned and ran out of the room.

II

I have been through the gates:
I have groped, I have crept
Back, back. There is **DUST**
IN THE STREETS, AND BLOOD....

CHARLOTTE MEW

"You certainly can lie like a rug!" Lillian said half admiringly. For the umpteenth time that day she had listened to plump, pleasant Gertrude, arbiter of the switchboard on the third floor of the Mammoth Writers' Building, as she told somebody at the other end of the line that Mr Josef was working at home today.

"Why don't you break down and tell 'em the truth?" Lillian demanded. "Why don't you say he's in Good Sam Hospital with the screaming what-have-yous?"

Gertrude only smiled. For some time she had been acting as house mother to a menagerie of Mammoth writers and she was necessarily the custodian of many secrets. Her world consisted of this little office with its switchboard and stationery cabinet, with a view only of the upper half of the elevator door across the hall, but very little went on in the building—or, for that matter, in the studio—that she did not know about.

"Those hoodlums, Dobie and Stafford!" Lillian went on virtuously. "Setting fire to people!"

"Listen, dearie," Gertrude told her. "Dobie and Stafford are your bosses. And they're one of the highest-paid writing teams in the business. When you get more than fifteen hundred a week you're not a hoodlum—you're the life of the party." Suddenly Gertrude noticed a fresh slip pinned under one slot in the tier of mailboxes. "What's this, somebody new?"

"Oh, I most forgot. While you were out to lunch the front office sent over a new Nincom writer. I meant to tell you. Somebody I never heard of—probably an importation from back East. Looks just the type to write purple passion stories." Lillian lighted a cigarette. "I put her in 303."

Gertrude smiled. "Another sob sister?"

"That's her. She looks like a mixture of Edna May Oliver and Charlotte Greenwood. . . ."

"With just a dash of Hedy Lamarr, I trust?" spoke a quick, excited voice from the hall.

Lillian blushed fiery red, but Miss Hildegarde Withers was not interested in apologies. "Now, don't get hysterical," she advised them. "Just do as I say. Put through a call to the police and tell them that there is a dead man in the office next to mine."

They gaped at her.

"Must I spell it for you?" snapped the schoolteacher. "A d-e-a-d man!"

In the room where the dead man lay the swift twilight of southern California deepened, casting into heavier shadow the faces of those who watched. Now the studio medico, a wizened little man in a crumpled white jacket, was squatting on his hunkers beside the body. Dr Evenson would have felt more at home back up the studio street in his neat little infirmary with its normal routine of cut thumbs and smashed toes and minor burns afflicting the army of Mammoth workers.

"Nothing I can do," he declared. "He's dead all

right." Dr Evenson rose to his feet and seemed to feel that his verdict lacked emphasis, for he repeated it. "Dead!"

Somebody finished it for him: ". . . my lords and gentlemen, stilled the tongue and stayed the pen"—in a low whisper. It was only the hatchet-faced woman who had discovered the body and who now lurked behind the tennis umpire's chair in the corner.

Burly Tom Sansom, built like a brick icehouse, stood by the door with his thumbs hooked into his Sam Browne belt and a scowl on his face. As chief of the Mammoth police force his duties were ordinarily confined to keeping children with autograph books from sneaking through the gates and to confiscating candid cameras on the studio sets. But he took this in his stride.

"All right, Jack," he ordered, turning to the other uniformed man behind him. "You and the doc better take him downstairs. The ambulance is at the back door." It was all over as easily as that.

But not for the lady in the corner. "I'm not one to speak out of turn," put in Miss Hildegarde Withers, "but isn't this a matter for the police?"

"Lady," Sansom explained wearily, "I *am* the police! The studio pays my salary, but I'm a sworn member of the police force of the city of Los Angeles. Just like a guard in a bank is. I'll make a report of this accident at the proper time."

"Accident?" Miss Withers sniffed.

Sansom winced. His assistant and the doctor who had been attempting to lift the body of Saul Stafford onto a stretcher now stopped and stared up at him, suddenly uncertain.

"That's what I said. Plain as the nose on your face." Miss Withers' head reared a little higher at the metaphor, but he went on. "Look, lady. Stafford was trying to tack up that poster onto the ceiling and, not being able to reach it, he tried to stand on the arm of that desk chair. The chair bucked and threw him and he was unlucky enough to light with his neck twisted. See?"

"That's about it, Chief," chimed in Dr Evenson. Not without some pushing and hauling the two men finally raised their grim burden and carried it out through the door, Saul Stafford's own overcoat covering him.

Sansom faced Miss Withers. "Like this!" He placed his thick hand on the back of the righted chair and pushed so that the chair leaned and then popped back upright with a jerk.

She still looked doubtful. "A man could hardly fall that far and that hard without making a noise that would wake the dead."

"Look, lady." Sansom's official politeness was curdling. "It doesn't mean anything that you didn't hear a noise. Your phone could've been ringing or you could've dozed off to sleep." He jerked his thumb toward the wall. "These offices are pretty well soundproofed, you know."

"I'm not the only person on this floor. Besides, suppose I were to tell you that earlier this afternoon Stafford hinted to me that he was afraid of somebody?"

"Huh? Oh, half the writers in this town are screwy. They got delusions, roaring d.t.s and so forth." He edged her politely toward the door. "Thank you very much, Miss Withers."

But she was not so easily convinced. "One moment, please. Will you do something for me? Just to make sure that this was an accident will you stand on that chair and jump off?"

Chief Sansom stared at her blankly. She told him, "Oh, I don't mean on the back or arm of the chair, just on the seat. And don't fall head first."

"I get it," he said doubtfully. "You want me to re-enact the thing and see how much noise it makes. Why——?"

"I want to find out whether anybody in the neighboring offices will hear you," she admitted. "It might settle this whole question once and for all."

He hesitated. "Okay, I guess." But he gave her a sidelong glance which made it clear that he thought she was as crazy as a bedbug. "Here goes." As ponderously as one of Ringling's brown elephants mounting a pedestal drum in the middle of the center ring Chief Tom Sansom climbed into the teetery swivel chair. He poised there a moment, obviously anxious not to re-enact the passing of Saul Stafford with too much exactness.

Then he jumped, landing flat-footed like a ton of brick. His thud shook the room and tipped over half the gadgets on the desk and tables. So far so good. But for scientific purposes the test was an utter failure. Before the acoustics could be tested in so far as to their effect on the other offices of the floor Sansom's voice rose in a mighty wail of anguish. "O-o-o-o-ow! Hell's bells and panther tracks! What the blazing, blooming, bloody hell——"

He was wildly hopping up and down on one foot, holding the other tenderly in his hands, while Miss Hildegarde Withers covered her maidenly ears. She watched as he ruefully pulled a thumbtack from the sole of his shoe, a thin and well-worn sole. It was one of the thumbtacks with which, according to his own theory, Saul Stafford had been engaged in fastening up the poster of Josephine Baker.

That did it. Soundproofed walls or not, there was now an excited concourse of voices in the hall. The door opened, disclosing a huddle of curious faces. The denizens of the third floor had finally come to the conclusion that something was up. They wanted to know what, and the air was blue with question marks.

"All right!" Sansom was insisting. "Mr Stafford just had an accident, that's all."

It was Frankie Firsk, he of the cropped hair and gnawed fingernails, who got in the first word. He took a quick bite at his forefinger and said, "Staff had an accident? I thought the accidents always happened to *other* people!" He almost snickered.

"It was the gas heater, wasn't it?" Melicent Manning pushed forward with a jingling of bracelets. "These offices are nothing but lethal gas chambers, that's what I say!"

"No, Miss Manning, it wasn't the gas heater!" snapped

Sansom. He forgot for a moment that she was the "Grand Old Lady" of the films. "Mr Stafford just had a fall."

"Where is he now?" Willy Abend, the wasp-waisted gentleman in the green suit, now pushed forward. "What happened? I want to know!"

"Back to your offices, everybody!" Sansom was getting near the end of his temper. "All right, all right——"

"Don't you shove me!" Abend cried. "This isn't Imperial Russia. I'm a U.S.A. citizen and I've got the Bill of Rights behind me and——"

"Oh, for God's sake!" exploded Tom Sansom.

Doug August, the young man Miss Withers had seen coming out of Nincom's office with clenched fists, now clenched them again. "Saul's dead, isn't he?" he said soberly. "I thought I heard them carry something heavy down the hall."

"Now if you'll all just go back to your offices..." Sansom tugged at his belt. "Just because a man has an accident does everybody in the hall have to butt in?" He indicated the door. "Now get moving, please."

He discovered that Miss Hildegarde Withers was tugging at his sleeve. "If everybody on the floor is here," she suggested, "why not ask them whether or not they heard the crash? I mean the first one?"

"Huh? I don't see..." But Sansom couldn't think of a reason for refusing. It developed that from the eight writers' offices in this hall six persons had come running at the sound of his crash or his voice. There was no telling which. Evidently the sound had not traveled beyond Gertrude's office into the other wing, which narrowed things down considerably.

"Okay," said the chief. "You can all help if you will. Take the offices in order. Who's in 301?"

Frankie Firsk pleaded guilty. No, he had heard nothing out of the way. "But I was reading poetry out loud to myself," he admitted. "Eliot's *Wasteland*. It always makes Hollywood seem sort of bearable...."

"Three o three?"

That was Miss Withers' office, and she had said her say.

"Three o five? Oh, that's this one. Well, who's in 307?"

Lillian, the lush and bedizened, spoke up from the fringe of the little group. "That's Mr Josef, but he isn't in the studio today. He's down at the Good Samaritan Hospital for his nerves. He——"

"Okay, okay. Now, across the hall. Who's got 308?"

That was Abend. The dapper playwright swore that he had heard no suspicious sound all afternoon. "Of course, I did have my radio on. Clara and I were listening to the police calls."

Clara, a vague and adipose member of the secretarial staff, was in agreement. Long since she had ceased to wonder at the vagaries of writers and if Mr Abend wanted the police calls taken down in shorthand she took them. "It's for the radio play I'm doing on the side," Abend told them defiantly. "I'm gathering color. I want to do something with real social significance."

"Okay." Sansom cut him short. "Three o six?"

Lillian spoke up again. "That's Mr Dobie's office. I work for him and Mr Stafford. But Mr Dobie wasn't in all afternoon—he's out on the set."

"Oh, he is?" Sansom frowned.

"Mr Dobie usually goes out and watches them shooting when he hasn't an assignment," Lillian said. "Gertrude is trying to get him on the phone now, but you can't interrupt a scene, you know."

"All right. Number 304?"

"That's mine," spoke up Melicent Manning. "But I'm afraid I was so busy trying to devise a scene where Deanna gets passionately kissed and still stays sweet sixteen that I didn't pay any attention to any noises. When I write I just lose myself!"

Chief Sansom muttered something under his breath. "Okay. Three o two?"

Doug August said that with the antique typewriter he

had been issued he couldn't hear the crack of doom. "It makes more noise than a machine gun, and I didn't let it cool off all afternoon. I've got to get a whole sequence out for Mr Nincom before he leaves for Arrowhead tomorrow. And if you don't mind, I'll get back to it." He turned and shouldered his way through the crowd, the others eddying after him. Sansom worked them all through the door and leaned against it.

"That's the list," he told Miss Withers. "So..."

"So not one person heard the crash when Saul Stafford fell. And you still insist he had an accident."

"Well, it stands to reason."

There was a commotion in the hall, and then the door was shoved open by a vast, gargantuan man with heavy, slashed eyebrows and the wide, innocent eyes of a child. "I'm Dobie, Virgil Dobie!" he cried. "Where's Saul? What's all this about? If it's a gag it isn't funny."

"Your collaborator has been taken away in an ambulance," Miss Withers told him. "With a broken neck."

His face went chalky gray, and Dobie felt for a chair.

"He's at Lumsden Mortuary Haven, on Western," Chief Sansom said. "I'm sorry, Mr Dobie."

Virgil Dobie wasn't listening. Miss Withers thought that he looked like a man desperately frightened, frightened for his own skin. "The chief here thinks that it was an accident," she told him. "He thinks that Stafford broke his own neck while standing on a chair to tack up that poster. But I was in the next office and I'm not so sure."

Dobie looked up at the ceiling, frowned, and then turned toward Miss Withers. Something seemed to be puzzling him.

"I've got to run along and report this thing," Sansom said briskly. "But I've one last word before I go." His finger wagged in Miss Withers' face. "If it wasn't an accident on account of nobody heard him fall, then how could it have been—well, been anything else?"

"Such as *murder?*" she prompted softly.

He nodded. "You think that a fight in which one guy

could break another guy's neck wouldn't make more noise than any fall?"

Miss Withers considered that. "You mean that in disproving your own case I've wrecked my own too?"

"That's exactly what I mean!" insisted Chief Sansom. "So put that in your pipe and smoke it." He went out of the room and slammed the door.

Dobie stood up as if about to follow. "One moment," Miss Withers said. "I'm a stranger here and I'm being Mrs Buttinsky. But there's a hole in the chief's theory, a hole as wide as a house." She looked up at the dangling poster again.

"I think I know what you mean," Virgil Dobie admitted. "You think it was a frame." His thick, angled eyebrows went up half an inch.

She nodded. "Why should a man stand on a teetery chair to tack up a poster that was already firmly tacked to the ceiling when I came into this office earlier this afternoon? —answer me that."

He couldn't. "Say," Dobie thrust, "you aren't——? I mean, *you* couldn't be the sleuth I read about in the *Reporter*?"

"Perhaps I am. At any rate, I walked into something that smells. Tell me—you knew Mr Stafford better than anybody else—who would have a reason for murdering him?"

Dobie didn't answer. He was staring at her. "I thought you'd be—well, different."

"Never mind that. Who could have murdered your partner?"

"Nobody. Nobody at all," declared Virgil Dobie. "Saul lived alone in a little apartment crowded with pipes that he never smoked and books that he never read. He never chased the tomatoes—I mean girls. All he liked to do was eat and drink. And have laughs."

"Did anybody ever threaten him, to your knowledge?"

"Anybody? You mean everybody! Half the people in Hollywood have threatened to break both our necks at one time or another but they always cool off. You see, Saul and I set out years ago to try to keep Hollywood from taking itself so seriously. Nobody ever murders on account of a practical joke."

Miss Withers said, "No? You never know just how people will react when their toes are well stepped on. And remember, young man, if Stafford was murdered, as I think, then the killer presumably has exactly the same motive for murdering you!"

He stared at her as if the thought were not new to him. "Somebody among the victims of the practical jokes you two loved to play has taken it the wrong way," she went on. "Where are you going, Mr Dobie?"

He barely paused. "If I had any sense maybe I'd take a quick powder and grab the first plane for New York. But I suppose I'll just rush out and lap up some sauce. There's quite a bit of courage in a bottle of dark Jamaica rum."

"You're not frightened, Mr Dobie?"

"I think I am," he told her gravely. "It could be."

"Wait!" she cried. "Won't you help me try to find the killer?"

"If what you say is true," Virgil Dobie called over his shoulder, "then I won't need to. He'll find me!" And, grinning, he was gone.

Miss Withers sat and waited. At six o'clock Gertrude Lafferty tapped at her door to tell her that it was time to close up the switchboard. "Are you going to stay late tonight?" she asked.

"I don't know," said the schoolteacher slowly. She had a sudden hunch that Gertrude was thinking things that she was not willing to say, that she was more than normally interested in Miss Withers' own plans for the evening.

Perhaps this was the worm on the hook. During the past hour or so the schoolteacher had purposely been making noises like a detective, had pretended to be sure Saul Stafford was murdered when no one could be sure of anything. All that would be very likely to force someone's hand. Since she was so determined to prove it a murder, a likely suspect might be handed her. She waited eagerly.

"Because if you *are* going to stay late," Gertrude went on, "I can leave you a night line through to the main switchboard. It's no trouble at all."

That was not the kind of a line Miss Withers hoped for, and she indicated as much.

"Well—good night!" And Gertrude was gone.

"There is a young woman who will bear watching," decided the schoolma'am. She sat at her desk, staring at the photograph of tired calla lilies which ornamented the opposite wall. Outside her Venetian blinds the twilight had deepened into black velvet night, a night shot with stars that were pale and wan above the wagging searchlights and the glaring neon signs of Hollywood.

Long ago, she supposed, the others had gone their separate ways. But she chose to sit here alone, with only one shaded light on her desk, alone with the ghostly presence of Saul Stafford who had not wanted to die. It was at once the most perplexing and the most poignant problem that Miss Withers had ever faced. Stafford had half turned to her as one human being to another. Her hands had been tied at the moment by a mistaken sense of loyalty to her employer. Otherwise Stafford might be alive at the moment.

It was a challenge that she must face. Murder next door, murder a few feet away from her. . . .

For murder it must be. In spite of the tipped chair, in spite of the carefully arranged picture created by dangling poster and spilled thumbtacks, she could not believe that Saul Stafford had met death by misadventure.

She took up her letter to the inspector again, feeling the need of talking to someone. There was an element of humor, she realized, in her turning to him. Never once in the many times they had crossed paths on the murder trail had she failed to wish audibly that he was far away so that she might have a free hand. And now she had it.

The little wire terrier of an Irishman was three thousand miles away, and she had no one to argue with. It was not easy to form her thoughts without putting them into words.

So she tapped busily away on the keys of the typewriter for a few minutes, describing the hilarious descent of Chief Sansom upon the thumbtack. Then she stopped, her fingers poised above the keys, listening, not only with her ears, but with every pore of her body.

Somebody was in the hall outside her door, somebody who had walked as softly as a cat. Somebody was breathing out there now, breathing and waiting. . . .

Mis Withers started to reach for the telephone. Then she realized that the line was dead. Quickly she rose to her feet and tiptoed across the room to the hatrack. With her black cotton umbrella gripped firmly in her hand, she approached the door. Forcing herself to take long, silent breaths, she reached out toward the knob. A quick pull at the door, and whoever was waiting on the other side might be jerked forward, surprised and off balance. She could get in at least one good crack with the umbrella which lent itself both to bludgeoning and stabbing.

"One—two—three!" she whispered softly, and jerked. There was nobody at all in the hall.

Miss Hildegarde Withers was not one to hold with ghosts and apparitions except in an extremely figurative sense. It was all right to imagine the ghostly presence of a murdered man standing invisibly behind her as she sought to avenge him. But ghosts who listened and breathed in doorways . . .

This ghost was now fumbling about in the office across and down the hall—306 it was. She could hear the faint creak of a drawer, the rattle of glass on metal. There was a faint luminous wavering, like a giant glowworm, beyond the frosted pane of the door.

"Ghosts do not breathe and they do not rattle drawers," the schoolteacher sensibly decided. "And anyone who has a right to be in that room would turn on the light in a normal fashion. Ergo and ipso facto, I have the murderer trapped. Maybe."

Gripping her umbrella firmly in her hand, she tiptoed down and tried the knob of 306. It was locked on the inside. Then she saw the faint light inside die away. For a moment she thought that she had been heard, but then there was a scraping sound and the flare of another match. And still the faint rattling and shuffling.

Miss Withers waited, her lips pressed grimly together. Then a drawer banged shut inside, and someone came toward the door with quick, nervous steps. She readied her weapon.

The door opened, and the schoolteacher started a haymaker. She managed to pull the punch, however, in the nick of time. For it was Lillian, the lush and bedizened Lillian, who came rushing out of the office. She opened her mouth as if she contemplated a good, rousing scream.

"Don't!" said Miss Withers sharply. The mouth stayed open. "What were you doing in Virgil Dobie's office?"

"Why! I have a perfect right——" Lillian burbled. "I work for Mr Dobie and Mr Stafford."

"Do you always work in the dark?" pressed Miss Withers. "What were you after? I judge that you didn't find it, as your hands are empty."

"None of your business!" the girl snapped.

"I'm afraid it is. Of course, if you'd rather I called Chief Sansom . . ."

"Call ahead." For some reason Lillian was amused.

"Or the regular police perhaps?"

Lillian said nothing, but her dark eyes were warier. The schoolteacher took her arm. "Child, this is no time for such goings on. You didn't kill Saul Stafford. Why try to protect the one who did?"

"Protect?" the girl gasped. "Do you think I'm crazy? I'm not protecting anybody. I sneaked back here to look for something in Mr Dobie's desk. Something that I thought would maybe be——I mean——"

"Come on into my office and tell me all about it,"

pressed Miss Withers, trying hard not to sound too much
like a police matron on a juvenile delinquency case.
Lillian suffered herself to be led inside, took a chair and
lighted a cigarette, but there was still considerable resistance in the square of her shoulders and the set of her
lower lip.

"I'm not just being meddlesome," Miss Withers
explained. "But you've probably heard by now who I am,
and a thing like this is naturally a challenge. If Mr Stafford
was murdered right under my nose I want to find out why
and by whom. I'm a fine technical expert on murder if I
can't solve one next door. As one woman to another, won't
you help me?"

Lillian frowned. "Are you really a detective?"

Miss Withers nodded. "Detectives, like murderers,
often look like quite ordinary people. Now what were you
looking for in Virgil Dobie's office?"

Lillian said, "You're not interested in the reward, if
there is one? You wouldn't——"

"I'll not contest it with you," said the schoolteacher,
amused. "Provided there is one. Sometimes there isn't,
you know."

Lillian's deep eyes shone. "But sometimes there is!
And I need the money. With money I can get hairdress-
ers, costumers, voice coaches—maybe a nose operation. I
can have screen tests made!"

"I see," said Miss Withers. "What was it you hoped to
find in Dobie's office? Was it evidence that he killed Saul
Stafford by any chance?"

That was a shot in the dark and it missed clean.
Lillian looked confused. "What? Oh no, nothing like that.
But I just remembered something I'd seen when I was
filing some of Mr Dobie's personal papers. I think that
both he and Mr Stafford were being blackmailed!" Lillian
lowered her voice. "Because when I helped make out
their income-tax reports last year I know that Mr Stafford
reported over three thousand dollars in bad debts, all
loaned to the same person. And the other day, in Mr

Dobie's personal file, I found an I.O.U. for two thousand dollars signed by that same man—and a canceled check for five thousand dollars that had been paid to him!"

Miss Withers digested that. "Blackmailers don't give I.O.U.s as a rule. Or accept checks. But it might be a lead. Was that what you were looking for just now?"

Lillian nodded. "I thought maybe—about the reward, like I told you. But the I.O.U. and the canceled check are gone." She was looking at the toe of her slipper.

"And the name of the man?"

"I don't remember." Lillian frowned. "It was Dick——"

"Come, come—you remember something about it. Was it a long name? Was it Smith or Jones or——?"

"It was Laval, I think. Something like that. But the stuff was gone, I tell you!" Lillian was breathing hard now and about ready to snap. So the schoolteacher waved her away.

"Thank you very much," she said. "For nothing," she added after the girl was gone.

Things were beginning to happen though. The schoolteacher began to whistle a little tuneless tune. Lillian had built up a very nice straw man. Suspect Number One, the well-known straw man about town, Mr Dick Laval. Even the name was artificial sounding.

Long since Miss Withers had learned to beware of the Greeks bearing gifts. She had also discovered that the police were more or less right in never paying any attention to information that they did not have to drag out of an unwilling witness.

It *was* murder! Her feeling was more than a hunch. Of course, there remained the pressing problem of the "how." Necks, she thought, must be rather difficult to break. It would take a bit of doing, as the Britishers say. In fact, she could not remember another case in which death had been brought about in just that way. Or was there one long since and far away?

She worried that problem as a cat worries a ping-pong ball across a carpet all the way out of the darkened studio, kept it tossing in the air as she rode back to town in a taxi. It was a long haul, and she decided that it might be a good idea to seek closer lodgings.

But there was time enough for that later. Now she studied her problem through a trayful of dinner in her hotel room. Somehow Saul Stafford had been murdered. He had feared auto accidents and poison in his drinking water and instead had received a neatly broken neck. Miss Withers tried to remember about the classic murder methods. The thuggees of India, for instance. They used a silken noose, didn't they?

But all this wasn't getting her anywhere. There was one last resort. She picked up the phone and asked the operator to connect her with Spring 7-3100. "In New York City," she hastily added, and sat down to wait.

Three thousand miles away a wiry, grizzled little Irishman spoke a weary "Hello" into the phone.

"I'm delighted to find you at your office, Oscar!" came the voice of Hildegarde Withers.

"I'm not at my office," he told her. "I'm home and supposed to be asleep. But some fool down at headquarters relayed your call. What in heaven's name are you up to now?" He yawned noisily.

"Listen carefully," she cried across the miles of wire. "Have you got a pencil?"

"Hildegarde! I know that old gag. I say, 'Yes,' and then you say, 'Well——'"

"This is no gag. Oscar, I want you to have one of your men look through the files down at headquarters and see if there's ever been a homicide case where the victim's neck was broken without any marks and without any noise. If you find one, for heaven's sake, wire me how it was done."

Inspector Oscar Piper scratched his hairy chest through the gap in the front of his rumpled pajamas. Then he reached for the dead cigar that lay in the ash tray on his bed table.

"Oscar? Are you going back to sleep?"

"I'm thinking. Wait a minute, will you? About eight

years ago, maybe nine. Berry... Ferry... Ferris... Harris—
that's it. Emily Harris."

"She killed somebody that way?"

"No, Hildegarde. The Harris dame was a fat blonde
living down in Greenwich Village. In those days the
village was something. Artists and musicians and old maids
of both sexes, well steeped in gin. Anyway, the Harris gal
was found early one morning by the milkman or the paper
boy or somebody, lying in a soft flower bed with her neck
broken. It was only about five feet below her bedroom
window."

"But how was it done?"

"There you got me," the inspector was forced to
confess. "The fall didn't seem hardly enough to snap her
neck, so the case is still in our 'Open' file. There was a
drunken brawl in her studio that night, and all that the
other guests could tell us was that she had complained of a
headache and gone to bed. We held her boy friend for a
day or two but we had to let him go for lack of evidence."

Miss Withers almost forgot to breathe. "Oscar, what
was the boy friend's name?"

"Oh—Demarest or Levy or something. Why? He was
a phony poet, a skinny guy with a beard."

"The name couldn't have been Laval, could it?"

"That's right! Then you did remember the case after
all! It was Derek Laval." The inspector pushed his cigar to
the far corner of his mouth. "Hello? Hello, Hildegarde?"
He rattled the receiver against the hook. "Hello! Operator, on that call from Hollywood you cut me off!"

III

Death is an angel with two faces:
to us **HE TURNS A FACE OF TERROR,**
Blighting all things fair....

THEODORE C. WILLIAMS

"I said nix on Myrna Loy," roared Mr Thorwald L. Nincom into the telephone. "Sam, I don't care a hoot what Metro is willing to trade her for. She can't play Lizzie Borden. Maybe five years ago, before they sweetened her up into the perfect wife for Nick Charles, but not now. Nor Dunne either. The fans won't take it."

He listened for a moment, riffling through the stack of unopened morning mail on his desk. "Who? Darnell? Of course Linda is cute as a bug but she's too damn starry eyed. No, I've sent for Gaynor, and we're going to take some tests. And then I'm off for Arrowhead until the end of the week. Oh, look, Sam—one more thing. You might drop the word to stenographic that Miss Madison, Miss Jill Madison, would be happier in some other line of work outside the studio. She was my secretary up to yesterday but she's got no sense of loyalty. You'd think she was doing you a favor by working for you. I've been a father to the girl, and what did I get for it?"

Sam Lothian, executive vice-president of Mammoth, hung up the phone with a smile, having heard through the

38

studio grapevine exactly what Mr Nincom had got for it. He made a note on his desk pad: "Tell Louie B. no dice on Loy" and, beneath it, "Ax for Madison."

Then he pressed a buzzer and said, "Send Miss Withers in. And get Sansom over here."

He leaned back in his chair, the perfect picture of a banker about to refuse a loan, a bald, plump, prosperous banker in an unprosperous community. Or so Miss Hildegarde Withers decided when she was ushered into his august presence.

"I suppose, Miss Withers," he began pleasantly, "you are wondering why I asked you to come over to my office first thing this morning, eh?"

"Not at all," returned that lady. "You are about to tell me to mind my own business."

Sam Lothian gulped. "Er-r-r, yes. I mean—well, I understand that criminology is an avocation of yours. You've made rather a hobby of homicide."

"I have. And I can smell murder a mile away."

"Sometimes, perhaps, when it isn't there. The way some overzealous doctors always rip out your tonsils or your appendix just because they like to operate?"

The schoolteacher failed to see any connection. "Murder is murder, and it can't be hushed up."

"The trouble with a hobby," said Lothian with a pained look, "is that we all have a tendency——" He looked up. "Oh, come in, Tom. You know Chief Sansom, don't you, Miss Withers? I was just saying that the trouble with a hobby is that we all have a tendency to ride it too much. You, Miss Withers, have a hunch that a member of our writing staff did not die an accidental death last night, a hunch as yet unsupported by evidence. By the way, have you talked to any newspapermen?"

She shook her head, and the tension in the office lessened a fraction. Lothian looked at Chief Sansom who was teetering on the edge of his chair and nodded.

"Really, there can be no question of hushing anything up," he continued. "A full report of the accident was made to the police last night. I have here"—and he picked up a sheet of paper—"I have a copy of the preliminary postmortem report which is being filed by Doctor John Panzer, chief coroner of the city of Los Angeles. He says: 'I have made a complete examination of the cadaver of Saul Stafford at Lumsden Mortuary Haven, 1243 Western Avenue. Results as follows: Anterior surface of body—negative.' That means no bruises. 'Abdominal cavity—negative to all poisons except ethyl alcohol. Cranial cavity—negative except to ethyl alcohol, concentration of 0.184.' That means he was moderately tight. 'Skeletal structure—a fracture dislocation of the second cervical vertebra and lesion of the spinal cord. Conclusion: Death from brain coma and/or lung asphyxia caused by break in spinal cord, either of which alone would be sufficient to cause death. There are no evidences of violence or of suicidal intent.' All symptoms listed are entirely compatible with the theory of *death by misadventure.*' So you see, Miss Withers——"

"Stafford was about two thirds swacked and he fell offen a chair and busted his neck," Sansom put in heavily.

"I'm telling you this, Miss Withers, because we want you to be perfectly satisfied," Lothian continued. "Doctor Panzer is an experienced and conscientious man." He rose to his feet. "And I might also point out to you that in the forty-some years since the motion-picture industry moved to California there has been no major crime committed inside the walls of any studio!"

"There's a first time for everything," said the schoolteacher doggedly. But she was on the spot and knew it. "Of course," she reminded them, "there is the fact that I had a talk with Stafford before he died and he told me he was afraid of being murdered. . . ."

"A coincidence," Lothian told her. "If he wasn't pulling your leg. The man had a mania for playing practical jokes and ribbing people, you know."

"But death had the last laugh," pointed out Miss Withers tartly, and made her exit.

If the front-office nabobs had a tendency to take the

demise of Saul Stafford somewhat lightly, it was not a feeling shared on the third floor of Writers' where very little work was in progress that morning. In Gertrude's office there was a gathering of the secretaries, Lillian and fat Clara and one or two others, all talking a blue streak and reading the morning papers.

The Stafford story was on page nineteen of the *Times* whose modest one-column head was "ACCIDENT FATAL TO SCENARIST." Even the *Examiner* went no further than "DEATH DRAWS CURTAIN ON PLAYBOY WRITER'S MADCAP LIFE." Both papers discreetly omitted the name Mammoth, saying only "a major studio."

"Take it easy, Lil," Gertrude said. "They didn't even mention your name."

"There are a lot of things that didn't get into the paper," Lillian said sharply.

"And that won't, dearie," Gertrude interposed. She looked up as the elevator door clanged and Miss Hildegarde Withers came up to the window. Then she carefully wrote down "10:35 A.M.—Withers in."

"Good morning," greeted the schoolteacher. "By the way, do you keep a record like that for everyone?"

Gertrude nodded. "It's a sort of studio rule. Not so much to check up on the hours people keep and how many callers they have as it is to have a record of where all writers are—in case the producer or supervisor wants to get in touch with them."

"You don't throw the sheets away, do you?" Miss Withers pressed on. "I was thinking particularly of yesterday afternoon." She suddenly lowered her voice, realizing that the secretaries were listening so hard that you could almost feel it. "Could I see that record?"

"I'm very sorry, Miss Withers, but——"

"It isn't just idle curiosity," insisted the schoolteacher. "It struck me that no one can come out of the elevator without being seen from where you sit. Nor can anyone come up the stairs and pass to any one of the offices in this wing. In other words, you have a complete check on everything."

"I'm sorry, but it's against the studio rules," Gertrude announced. "Besides, I've turned in the report to Mr Lothian."

"Thank you just the same," said Miss Withers, and started down the hall. The way lay clear before her with two approaches to the problem. She could, of course, attack it through the usual door of "who?" Who had opportunity, who had motive, who had the type of mind that would incline toward murder as the answer to an emotional impasse? Or she could come at it backwards through the personality of the victim.

She went into her own office, removed the top-heavy hat which was her trademark and placed it beside her umbrella. Then she crossed over to the connecting door. As she turned the knob the schoolteacher took a deep breath, steeling herself against what she was about to face. After all, the glorified junk shop was something of a shock to any sensitive nature. The dive into a dime museum, into a magpie's nest of small, bright objects, was not a thing to be taken lightly. But it was the back door to Stafford's mind, the way to an understanding of what he had been and why he met the end he did.

She came through the door, stopped short and for as long as one might have counted ten she stood, stiff and unbelieving. Then she reached for the telephone. "What's happened to this office?"

Gertrude finally understood. "Oh, the janitor always straightens up when a writer leaves. Everything personal was packed up last night."

Completely disconsolate, Miss Hildegarde Withers looked upon an office as neat and impersonal as a blank sheet of paper. Gone were the posters, gone the gadgets, gone the magpie's nest. And gone the clues, gone with the wind.

There was nothing, absolutely nothing, which carried any message for her. She looked all through the desk drawers, under and inside the blotting pad, everywhere. Once for a moment she thought that she had struck pay dirt, for on the margin of the desk blotter she found the scribbled notation, "Laval—Ox 7003." Eagerly she picked up the phone and asked to have the number dialed for her, but the ringing at the other end of the line was a curious double buzz, and the exchange operator finally cut in to say that Oxford 7003 had been discontinued.

Finally she abandoned the search and went back to her own office where she stared glumly at her desk and waited for a hunch. None came, but she had an interruption in the shape of Buster who entered, bearing a large sealed envelope with red "Important" stickers all over it.

"From Mr Nincom's office," he announced. "Say, Miss Withers, is it true what they're saying? That you're a detective and——?"

"I wonder," she said glumly. "I wonder if I'm a detective or a——Never mind." She shook her head. "By the way, how is the romance burgeoning? Did you follow my suggestion about dropping Confucious overboard?"

Buster's shoulders sagged. "I didn't have the chance. I mean, Jill is sort of out of reach right now. Confucius say, 'Girl who think about money have no time for think about love.'"

"Oh yes, the sweepstake thing. Well, she'll get over that."

"Maybe," he said doubtfully. "Maybe she'll get over it too quick. Because the drawing for the Irish Sweep doesn't take place for two weeks yet. So that cablegram from Dublin is a phony!"

"Does Jill Madison know that?"

He shrugged. "I'm not going to be the one to tell her!" And Buster departed. Miss Withers started to open the envelope.

After a few minutes she was interrupted by the telephone. It was her agent, the energetic Mr Wagman. "Just wanted to see if everything is okay," he queried. "I meant to drop in on you, but this Stafford tragedy has complicated matters. He was my best client, you know. Him and Dobie."

"Complicated?"

"Yeah. They had a contract as a team. Now there's only one of them. I'm trying to get Dobie kept on alone. If it fails it's for one reason. He's got a reputation as a trouble maker."

"Really?"

"Yeah. It doesn't pay in this business to make trouble. Such as"—here Wagman's voice dropped—"such as going around talking about murder and so on. You were hired for a different job, you know." His tone was friendly enough, but there was somewhere a subtle threat.

"Thank you," said Miss Withers gently, and hung up. Then she took up the sheaf of screen play which Nincom had sent her. She opened it, looked at the title, *Miss Lizzie Borden*, and at the long list of writers whose names had been set down as contributors. She read:

SEQUENCE "A"

Fade in:

Exterior Borden mansion—Full shot (Day)

A-1 *A big white mansión with white pillars, many porticoes, etc. In the b.g. is the Sound, with the masts of seven or eight of the Borden whaling fleet showing above the house. On the lawn are twelve or fifteen young people, all dressed in the costume of the Gay Nineties, playing a fast game of croquet. Foremost among them is* LIZZIE BORDEN, *young and lovely, the belle of the town. She suddenly turns and runs toward camera, laughing and following the ball.* JOHN ELLIS *follows her.*

A-2 *Closer shot—*LIZZIE *and* ELLIS

He is a tall, gay young blade. (Gary Cooper type)

He raises his mallet to hit the ball.

LIZZIE

(Frightened)

Oh no! Stop!

Camera pans down to close shot as Lizzie carefully brushes big blue butterfly from ball.

LIZZIE
(Reproachfully)
Ellis, you might have crushed it!
(To butterfly)
Go on, you lovely thing. . . .

Miss Withers pushed the script away. "Go on yourself," she muttered, remembering the town of Fall River as she knew it, remembering that narrow, proper little street on which stood the boxlike Borden house. Then there were the photographs of Lizzie herself, that tight-lipped, cold-blooded president of the Christian Endeavor Society. Belle of the town, indeed!

Miss Withers looked up suddenly to see that her door was being softly opened. Lillian entered on tiptoe, looking more lush and sultry than ever. Something had impelled her to wear black today, evidently out of respect for the dead, but the dress she had chosen was of the slinky cocktail variety, giving an extremely gala effect.

"I only have a minute," Lillian said. "Gertrude's gone to lunch, and I asked to spell her at the board again today. Just so I could copy this list off for you. She was lying when she said she didn't have it."

And she handed Miss Withers a hastily scrawled record of the comings and goings of the floor for yesterday afternoon. The schoolteacher brightened considerably. "And nobody comes in or out of the hall without being checked?"

"Nobody," Lillian said.

"Then if Stafford was murdered the murderer's name should be on this list."

"I—I guess so." Lillian was in a hurry to get away.

Once alone, Miss Hildegarde Withers bent over the list. It didn't matter what went on here before about three yesterday because that was the time when she had seen Stafford alive and reasonably well. That left approximately two hours.

Sometime in that hundred and twenty minutes Saul Stafford had died. According to the record, at three yesterday most of the writers of the floor had been in their offices. The only exceptions were Mr Virgil Dobie who was supposed to be out on the set watching the shooting of his latest picture and Mr Wilfred Josef who was supposed to be in Good Samaritan Hospital. She read:

P.M.
3:10—Mr Firsk in
3:18—Clara in for Mr Abend
3:40—Miss Withers phoned Mr Nincom
3:48—Mrs Firsk phoned in to Mr Josef (no message)
3:50—Mr Parlay Jones phoned Mr Dobie (call transf. Stage 4)
4:05—Mr Pape for Mr Abend
4:07—Mr August out (to hamburger stand)
4:12—Lillian in (to Mr Dobie's office)
4:15—Mr Wagman in for Mr Firsk
4:17—Clara out
4:20—Clara in
4:25—Mr Wagman out
4:27—Mr August in
4:34—Lillian out
4:35—Mr Pape out
4:38—Buster in (package for Miss W)
4:45—Buster out
4:57—Miss Withers called police (call trans. to Sansom)

The schoolteacher pondered over this chart for some time, coming at last to the unpleasant conclusion that at the hour when she knew Saul Stafford to have died almost any person on the floor could have killed him. Any person, that is, who knew how to break a man's neck without leaving a mark.

She put the list carefully aside for the moment. It was, she decided, lunch time. On her way down the hall Lillian gave her a conspiratorial wink. "Oh, there's a telegram for you, Miss Withers!" the girl cried after her, and thrust a yellow envelope under the window.

Miss Withers stared at it thoughtfully all the way down in the elevator. Because the envelope had been opened and very amateurishly stuck back together again.

It turned out to be from the inspector. Luckily he had used the code which Miss Withers had worked out for such occasions, a code resulting from the simple expedient of placing one's hands one space to the right on a typewriter keyboard. That made the first word, "Jsttod," spell "Harris." She read: HARRIS FILE SHOWS NO PHOTO OF LAVAL. HAVE FRAGMENTARY PRINT RECORD ONE FINGER. QUERIED DR VAN DONNEN WHO SAYS PRACTICALLY IMPOSSIBLE FOR EVEN STRONG MAN TO BREAK ANOTHER'S NECK. WOULD BE INTENSE STRUGGLE AND MARKED BRUISES. WHAT TREE ARE YOU BARKING UP? OSCAR PIPER."

"I only wish I knew," said the schoolteacher unhappily as she put the wire away in her handbag. If Dr Max Van Donnen said it would be practically impossible for anyone to break a man's neck, then it was practically impossible. Max knew, or he wouldn't be the greatest police laboratory expert in the country.

Somehow the urge to see the stars lunching in the studio commissary had left Miss Withers. She marched through the studio gates in search of a little sandwich stand that she remembered seeing across the street.

But it was no sandwich stand that caught her eye now. There was the usual panorama of cowboy bit players, tourists peering from their dusty Chevrolets with the Midwestern license plates, children with Brownies and autograph books. And there was Jill Madison.

Miss Withers had seen that girl very slightly, and never as she was now. Jill walked up and down in front of the studio gates, four paces north, turn, four paces south.

"Mercy me!" said the schoolteacher to herself. "Did you ever see a *scream* walking!" Because that girl was an unstable chemical combination about ready to explode. She was a coiled spring, a set trap. She was trouble on high heels.

Miss Withers came up beside her. "Good afternoon, my dear."

Jill Madison, neat as a pin in a cheap, smart blue suit and a bravely ridiculous jockey cap with a feather in it, stopped short. She flashed a mechanical smile and nodded.

The schoolteacher could think of half a dozen questions she would have liked to ask Miss Madison, but this was neither the time nor the place. She went on across the street. This was none of her business. Or was it? Anyway, when she had finished her "Fan Mail Special"—one stuffed lamb chop with tea or coffee, fifty-five cents—and come out into the sunlight again Jill was still doing her guard duty.

Wait! She had stopped.

An open Packard with a special Darrin body rolled up to the curb outside the main gate. Virgil Dobie started to slide out. That was as far as he got, because Jill caught him flat-footed, the palm of her hand meeting his cheeks with the hard, vicious snap of a .22 rifle.

Jill Madison began to call him things in a low but sincere tone. She must have picked up the words from Mr Nincom, the schoolteacher thought, and then of course rephrased them to advantage.

For a moment there were red handprints on Dobie's face, and then they were blotted out by a tide of blush red which worked up from his neck. He said something to the girl which she would not hear and which Miss Withers, however she might gape, could not.

Then Dobie caught Jill Madison by both wrists, dragged her into the car and drove off. It was all over in a moment, so quickly, indeed, that the loungers outside the studio gates barely saw that anything was wrong. Dobie had not wasted any time in nipping that scene in the bud, the schoolteacher acknowledged.

She would very much have liked to follow the red Packard, but there was no taxi in sight. So she went on inside the gates again.

Up on the third floor Gertrude was just taking over the switchboard from Lillian, and both of them were talking to a man who seemed to be terribly surprised at everything. That, she realized a moment later, was because he had no eyebrows or eyelashes and his little beard was only a ragged memory.

"Miss Withers, this is Mr Wilfred Josef," Gertrude said.

She shook a limp, damp paw. "I was just telling the girls," said Josef, "that I should have stayed in the hospital. Those nurses gave me a lot of new limericks. There's one about the young lady, named Lassiter, Who screamed when a man made a pass at her. . . ." He took out a cigarette. "And the young couple, named Kelly, who——"

"I beg your pardon?" said Miss Withers.

"Okay, okay," Josef told her. "But when I heard about old Stafford I started writing one on him. I mean a clean one. Listen. There was an old Stafford, named Saul, Who got killed, so they say, by a fall. He landed, by heck, on the back of his neck, And nobody minded at all!" Josef guffawed at his own composition. Then he started to light his cigarette, thrust the match from him with a shrill yelp.

"What's the matter?" Gertrude asked, wide eyed.

He put the cigarette down, unlighted. "Nothing. Just a sort of phobia or something, the doctor says. It may be a long time before I can light a cigarette. Guess I'll have to learn to chew, huh?"

His tone was light and gay. Too light and too gay, Miss Withers thought. "The burned child . . ." she quoted to herself, and quietly withdrew.

"Here's another," Josef was saying. "There was a young girl from Purdue, Who covered her——"

"I think maybe you shocked Miss Withers," Gertrude said, looking down the hall.

Far from being shocked, Miss Hildegarde Withers was at the moment intent upon breaking and entering. As she lingered in the office she had noticed the mark, "12:55—Abend out," on the pad. Dobie's office would be locked. But perhaps the connecting door would not be. Perhaps . . .

Mr Abend did not lock his office. Perhaps the room would stand some investigation, but there was no time for that now. She held her breath and tried the connecting door which must lead into Virgil Dobie's office. It was open.

She found herself in a room obviously arranged for a big man who liked to be comfortable. The easy chair was vast and upholstered in red leather, with a big footstool. The couch had a spring mattress and big pillows, well rumpled. There was a reflecting reading lamp, and on one wall a white square of silvered composition which she imagined was a projection screen. Beside that was a small blackboard on a stand, now washed clean. Another wall held a cork bulletin board pinned with numerous newspaper reviews of the pictures which Dobie and Stafford had written.

Miss Hildegarde Withers sat calmly down at the desk and started to snoop through Virgil Dobie's possessions. The flat top drawers showed only stationery, both the studio type and an expensive hot-press note paper. There was a big sheaf of unanswered mail, including a letter from some New York publisher reminding Dobie that they awaited with breathless anxiety the remainder of the novel he had promised them two years before. There was numerous correspondence in regard to the purchase of rare books and to the binding of other books, usually in full leather. There were numerous bills for camera equipment, clothes, liquor and so forth, but none was more than four weeks old.

Among the bills was a receipt from the Postal Telegraph Company to the amount of $23.25, covering a cable and remittance to Mr Eugene Gach, care of Mammoth Distributing Corporation, Dublin, Eire. There was a bank statement from the Security-First National showing that Mr Dobie had a cash balance of $14,889.43.

One drawer remained, a drawer containing folded copies of today's *Times* and *Examiner* and a cryptic sheet of blue paper on which someone had scrawled cryptic lines of figures. For a moment Miss Withers thought that she had stumbled upon a modern Rosetta stone. The sheet had been so folded, handled, tattered, that she thought it must be important and copied it off without the slightest idea of what it meant. She put down:

****Pix	Code	Put	Take
1		2	
2		2	
3		2	
1	2	(2)	
2	2	2	
3	2	2	
1	2	2	
2	8	4	
3	8	4	
1	12	6	
2	18	(8)	
3	18	8	
1	26	12	
2	2	2	
3	32	(16)	

That was the booty, that and an insurance policy which she found at the bottom of the drawer, a policy to the amount of five thousand dollars, with double indemnity for sudden death, on the life of Virgil Dobie. The agent's name was listed as Harry Pape, and the beneficiary was Saul Stafford.

There was certainly nothing bearing the name of Derek Laval. Perhaps, after all, Lillian had been telling the truth.

Miss Withers frowned. In spite of herself she could not get over the feeling that she was being blind to something right in front of her nose.

Of course there was the tobacco humidor, a vast earthenware container flanked by rows of pipes. Miss Withers gingerly lifted the lid and was immediately greeted by the loud and tinkling musical strains of "Smoke Gets in Your Eyes." She replaced it hastily.

At that moment the phone rang. She looked at it. If the inspector were here he would pick it up, pretend to be Virgil Dobie and hope for some bit of information to be dropped into his lap. Well, the inspector wasn't here. But she could try.

She picked up the phone, said "Hello!" in as gruff a tone as she could manage.

There was a long wait at the other end of the line. "Lillian?" said a man's voice, cautious and muffled. Hawaiian music came faintly.

"No, this isn't Lillian!" she said. "Is there a message?"

Another wait. "Just tell Mr Dobie that Laval called, Derek Laval." And the line clicked as he hung up.

Miss Hildegarde Withers sat back and thought that one out. The straw man was getting awfully real. He cashed checks and talked over the telephone. And he liked Hawaiian music.

Five minutes later Miss Withers was back in her own office, inditing a telegram to the inspector which, she thought, might make him put one of those long, greenish-brown cigars into his mouth hot end first. She wrote:

INSPECTOR OSCAR PIPER
HOMICIDE BUREAU CENTRE STREET NYC
DEREK LAVAL HAS COMMITTED ANOTHER IMPOSSI-

BLE MURDER. ALL I KNOW OF HIM IS HE SEEMS
FOND OF HAWAIIAN MUSIC AND BLACKMAIL. LET-
TER FOLLOWS.

                                    HILDEGARDE

She had barely finished putting this into code when
her door burst open, and in came the lush and livid
Lillian, her stocking seams crooked, her hair askew and
her lipstick smeared upward from one corner of her mouth
in a rakish and unhumorous grin.

"Listen!" the girl exclaimed. "Have you got that list I
gave you earlier?"

"Of course," said the schoolteacher. "Do you want it
back?"

"Do I!" snapped Lillian. "I want to add something."
She snatched up the piece of paper, and for a moment
Miss Withers thought that the girl meant to destroy it.

"What's all this about?" she wanted to know.

"What's it about? I'll tell you what it's about! Virgil
Dobie's gone and hired Jill Madison as his private secretary after the studio fired her. And he says that if they
won't pay her salary, he will! And I can just go back to the
department and take my chance on getting another writer
or just copying, copying all day long. . . ."

"But why?" Miss Withers asked, because she obviously was expected to do so. "Why did he?"

"How should I know?" Lillian's full lower lip curled.
"How should I understand anything a writer does! But if
he thinks I'm going to go on sticking up for him——" She
whirled on Miss Withers. "Virgil Dobie told you he didn't
come up into this building at all yesterday afternoon,
didn't he? I mean, until after the body was discovered?"

Miss Withers nodded. "He was out on the lot, or the
set, or whatever it is they call it. Where they make
movies."

Lillian nodded. "He was! But not all afternoon. He
came up because his tobacco pouch was empty and he
wanted to fill it. I was in his office, doing some filing, and

he came in and went right out again. So I guess that smashes his pretty little alibi!" She carefully inserted "4:18—Mr Dobie in" and "4:28—Mr Dobie out" on the list. "That's the way the original reads. But when I copied it off for you I left his name out. I was going to do him a favor!"

Miss Withers looked dubious. "You mean you think that Mr Dobie could have come into his own office, filled his tobacco pouch, crossed the hall and killed Mr Stafford and then gone back out to the set all in ten minutes?"

"I wouldn't know about that," Lillian said as she moved toward the door. "How long does it take to do a murder anyway?"

IV

Fear and amazement beat upon my heart,
Even as **A MADMAN BEATS UPON A DRUM....**

Thomas Heyward

Gertrude Lafferty sat alone in the little office beside the switchboard, chewing some rather tasteless caramels and thinking her own thoughts. They were not, it would appear, especially pleasant thoughts, judging by the expression she was wearing when Miss Hildegarde Withers dropped in for a chat.

"I wonder if you'd be willing to help me," said Miss Withers hopefully. "Please try, because, placed as you are here in the very nerve center of everything, you know what goes on."

Gertrude looked dubious.

"What I really want to know is, did Virgil Dobie come up here yesterday afternoon? At about four-eighteen?"

"I don't think I ought to talk about that," Gertrude objected. "Mr Stafford is dead, and no one can help him by making trouble."

"No? Well, remember, that if it was murder the murderer is right here among us. Walking up and down, smiling and saying good morning, maybe planning something else——"

Gertrude paled perceptibly. "I don't——"

"And, of course," Miss Withers prodded pleasantly, "you are in a certain amount of danger. Because you may know something, you may have overheard something through the switchboard that you don't even *know* that you know!"

The plump girl didn't say anything but she contrived to look a bit haggard.

"There is no safety for anybody once a murderer has killed and gone scot free. Because he always strikes again and again. . . ."

"Wh-what do you want to know?" Gertrude said weakly.

"About Mr Dobie?"

Gertrude nodded. "Yes, he came up yesterday. I don't know the exact time. He just yelled, 'Hello, Mother Goddam'—he always calls me that because I have charge of the secretaries—and went on down the hall. But he was only on the floor for a minute or two, and then he went right back to the set."

"A minute or two? You don't think it was longer?"

"Ten minutes maybe."

"Murders have been committed in less time than that," Miss Withers observed.

Gertrude's eyes widened. "Oh, but—but he couldn't have done that! He couldn't have—have done anything to Mr Stafford!"

"And why not? Just because the men were inseparable?"

"I don't mean that. But when Mr Dobie came out—he was filling that big meerschaum pipe, I remember—he stopped in the office here for a moment. Just to play a rib on Mr Stafford, like they were always doing. He had me call Stafford's phone and tell him that Mr Josef was coming after him with a baseball bat!"

The schoolteacher frowned. "Mr Stafford answered the phone—you're sure of that?"

"Sure I'm sure. Mr Stafford just laughed because he caught on it was a rib. I was giggling, I guess. Anyway, they both knew Mr Josef wouldn't hurt a fly, no matter how mad he got. You see, both Mr Dobie and Mr Stafford were sort of hilarious over the gag they'd played on Mr Josef the night before when they scared him. They were always calling each other up and leaving funny messages."

"I can imagine," said Miss Withers. "And when Dobie left to go back to the set you are willing to swear that Stafford was alive and well?"

Gertrude nodded, then: "Except for a headache. He said he had one of his roaring headaches and please leave him alone."

"I think I feel one coming on, myself," Miss Withers observed.

The girl was sympathetic. "Why don't you take the rest of the day off, Miss Withers? I don't think anybody would know. Your boss is up at Arrowhead, they say. So he won't be calling you."

"It's an idea," mused the schoolteacher. "It really is. I could slip away now and look for a place to live. The hotel isn't too conveniently located for me."

Gertrude, always helpful, said that it was possible to lease a house in Brentwood or Westwood for two hundred dollars a month. "Without a pool, of course." She hesitated. "I could get in touch with a real-estate agent that I happen to know, and——"

"Perhaps a house would be a bit more than I need," Miss Withers said. "Do you know of any furnished apartments that can be rented by the week?"

Slightly disappointed, Gertrude said that the town was full of them. "But the Laguna Plaza and the Pelham are close to the studio. There are three or four others on that street too."

Miss Withers made a careful note of it. "I think I will run along," she said. Gertrude wrote "3:15—Miss Withers out" on the pad. "By the way," added the schoolteacher, "if a Mr Derek Laval calls——"

Gertrude's head snapped around. "What?"

Afire with secret triumph, Miss Withers said casually, "Oh, do you know him?"

"Yes. I mean, not exactly. Is he a friend of yours?"

The schoolteacher shook her head. "I've never met him," she said. "But I've heard of him. What is he like?"

Gertrude looked at the switchboard. "Oh, just a Hollywood playboy, I guess. I've seen his name in gossip columns for getting into a fight at the Trocadero bar, and things like that. And—and one of my sister's girl friends picked him up at the Palomar one night last summer. That's where the kids go to jitterbug, you know. She said he was a good dancer but not so good on the way home. Just another wolf, I guess. The kid had to walk from Vermont Avenue to La Brea."

"The more I hear of Mr Laval the less I care for him," Miss Withers decided. Suddenly her voice trailed away. She was staring over Gertrude's shoulder through the window out into the hall. Across that window was moving something furry—something zoologically horrible, for there was a yellow feather growing out of the fur.

"Good gracious!" said the schoolteacher, pointing.

Gertrude looked. Then she leaped from her chair and rushed out into the hall where she came upon a small, brisk woman who moved awkwardly yet swiftly along on hands and knees.

"Mame!" Gertrude ordered. "None of that!"

The lady in the furry headpiece stood up, still clutching a heavy suitcase. She smiled a breezy smile. "Darn this hat," said Mame. "I'd have got past you if it weren't for this confounded feather."

"Outside!" Gertrude ordered. "I've had enough complaints from my writers about you bursting in without being announced."

"Business is business," said Mame. Then she caught sight of Miss Withers and instantly set upon her as a potential victim. The case snapped open, disclosing vast skeins of varicolored neckties.

"They've got Charvet and Sulka lashed to the mast, and only six dollars!" She whipped out a particularly striking number in brown and blue. "Want to get your boy

friend something exquisite in French ties? Or, if you
haven't got a boy friend, lure one with——"

"Outside!" Gertrude repeated. "And I mean it!"

Unabashed, Mame bade them good afternoon and
departed. "Her husband was a prop man here years ago,"
Gertrude explained. "So after he was killed in an accident
Mame took to peddling ties around the studio. Only
they've gone up in price from fifty cents to six bucks, and
Mame has to high-pressure it a bit."

"There's no man alive for whom I'd buy a six-dollar
tie," said the schoolteacher severely, and took her departure.

The list of apartments was in her handbag, but Miss
Hildegarde Withers let it stay there while she consulted a
Los Angeles telephone directory. No, there was no Derek
Laval. Possibly he had an unlisted number. She would
have liked to try a city directory, but there was none in the
little drugstore where she had stopped.

Well, there still remained the newspapers. After a
trip which seemed to take her in wide circles around
Robin Hood's entire estate a taxi deposited her outside the
gingerbread grandeur of the *Herald-Express* building. There
were bound copies of the paper in the lobby, and she
started methodically to read back through them. But the
search for the well-known needle in the haystack was
simple by comparison.

After half an hour of this she gave it up. Another and
a better idea suggested itself to her. She crossed to the
advertising department, pondered for a moment and then
gave orders for a "Personal" to be inserted in tomorrow's
paper and run until canceled. "Derek (Dick) Laval—please
communicate regarding settlement of an estate—Box . . ."

That was not entirely a fabrication. Saul Stafford's
estate must be settled. "And a murderer's hash, if possible," she told herself.

She started out of the newspaper office and then
stopped. "How stupid of me!" she said aloud, and headed
back to the elevators. The City Room was on the fourth
floor, and, from her reading of newspaper stories, she

realized that all she had to do was to march inside as if she had business there, find the morgue and read at her leisure everything that had been printed about the elusive Mr Laval.

Nobody stopped her. The City Room was calm, as one might expect of an afternoon paper at this hour. She even came upon the morgue without difficulty, saw the tall filing cases, cabinets and bookshelves bulging with yellow envelopes. A peaceful old man sat in a hard chair with his feet on a table, clipping things out of the last edition.

"May I have the file on Derek Laval?" requested Miss Withers briskly.

He looked at her, went back to his clipping.

"Laval, please!" she repeated. "May I have it?"

"Sure," he said. "But there's a formality or two first." She waited expectantly. "Yes," he said. "You got to go four years to some college and major in journalism. Then you got to get a job on your hometown newspaper and forget all the nonsense they taught you in college. Then you got to get two or three jobs on big-town papers and forget some more and finally you get a job on the *Herald*, and I'll be tickled pink to stop my work any time and go hunt up the stuff you want." He indicated the door with a long, skinny finger. "Until then, nix."

There was nothing left for Miss Withers to do but take a dignified departure. Or was there? She found a ten-dollar bill in her handbag, waved it thoughtfully. "If I could just have a look at that envelope," she mused. "Just a glimpse of a picture of this Laval person. . . ."

"Save your money," said the keeper of the files. "Any picture that appeared in this paper you can buy a print of it down at the INS office. Those news services keep all that stuff. And dollars is their price, not ten." He went on placidly clipping.

Miss Withers found the INS office. They had no pictures of Derek Laval. They thought that Acme might.

Acme didn't. But she could try AP.

"I'm getting warmer," said Miss Withers. So she was.

AP had Mr Laval down twice on their list. A young man searched through the files, finally produced two old prints. One was a flashlight picture of a police raid on the Swing Club, an emporium devoted to the sale of drinks after two-o'clock curfew, with a number of somewhat startled customers crowding out of the doorway. "DEREK LAVAL, LOCAL PLAYBOY, FLEES RAIDED HOT SPOT" was the caption. The picture was not too good, for the flashlight cast a glaring and unnatural light on the men in the doorway, and the one man who faced the camera, presumably Mr Laval, was holding his arm up in front of his eyes. He reminded Miss Withers of somebody she had met in the last day or two, but who it could be she had no idea.

The other picture was captioned "JIMMY GRANT SCORES WINNING GOAL FOR RIVIERA IN SPITE OF HEROIC RIDING OFF BY DEREK LAVAL." It showed two men on two galloping horses, both waving whippy polo mallets at a round ball which seemed to float in the air. The face of the farther man, who was trying to block the player with his pony, was turned so that the schoolteacher could see only that he wore dark glasses.

Miss Withers bought both pictures and carried them off with her. It was an odd, backhanded way to track down a murderer. But she felt that she was hot on the trail of the straw man, the little man who wasn't there. . . .

The taxicab carried her back toward Hollywood, winding its way through the mazes of Los Angeles streets, past the big open-front markets with their jeweled displays of shining fruits and vegetables, past the little junky mission-type bungalows, the boxes in stucco with near-Spanish lines and brilliant coloring, past new white apartment houses with formal gardens and oval swimming pools, past cocktail bars and churches with neon lights. . . .

Vast smooth boulevards that narrowed suddenly into little bottlenecked streets with car tracks, red lights and green lights and semaphores and amber lights . . .

And then Miss Withers chanced to see an apartment sign—"The Pelham." That had been one of the places on the list Gertrude gave her. On an impulse she had the driver pull up on the corner of Cowbell Canyon Drive. It was late in the afternoon, but haply not too late to see about arranging for a place to live.

The Pelham had no vacancies.

Down the street she saw the sign of Laguna Plaza. That was another on the list, she remembered. So she strolled along. The Laguna Plaza had only two apartments available, both with three bedrooms and with a lease desired.

So she went on along the pleasant drive with its towering palm trees which looked to the Manhattan schoolteacher as if they had been set out this morning and would be hauled away at any moment.

The apartments that she saw were all either unfurnished or else the halls smelled of cooking cabbage or else the living rooms had blind fireplaces and large imitation oil paintings of an evil-looking Spanish gentleman in a red ruff. All but the one on the corner—a pleasant-looking three-story building in a modified ranch-house style with a long balcony set with brightly colored pots stretching across the front.

Beneath the balcony was an archway, and one went through into a little garden with irregular walks, a fountain and an alcove for mailboxes. Miss Withers was looking for the bell marked "Manager" but even as her finger poised over the button she froze.

A sportsman would have said that the schoolteacher was pointing, and indeed her position was rather similar to that adopted by a bird dog.

Which was as it should be, for the second name at the top of the column was "Derek Laval."

When she left ten minutes later she was equipped with a receipt for a month's rent on a small "double" in the rear, a pleasant little two rooms and bath whose rent was only half again as much as she had intended to pay. The furniture and decorations resembled a slightly shopworn department-store window display, but it would do. She would have taken an apartment here if it had been furnished with camp stools and a hammock.

She also was equipped with a key and with the information—obtained with elaborate casualness—that the building had several tenants who were "in pictures" and that Mr Laval was a very nice man who always mailed his rent check regularly.

"I think I know him," the schoolteacher had said hopefully, watching the landlady with an eagle eye. "Isn't he a tall man with a limp and sort of an English accent?"

But Mrs Dermott had been vague about the description. "He isn't so tall," she said slowly. "Not so very. Anyway, I haven't seen very much of him since I took over the management here. He lives somewhere out in the San Fernando Valley, I think, and just uses this when he has to stay over in town."

That was as far as she had dared to go at the moment. But at least Miss Withers felt that she was nearing the end of the trail. She had been a neighbor of the murder victim and now she was moving into the same apartment house with the man she felt must be the killer.

Back at her hotel she paused at the desk to leave word that she was checking out. "Oh yes, Miss Withers," said the clerk. "The studio called you and wants you to call back."

She called the Writers' Building, but the main-studio operator told her that Gertrude had gone for the night. Then, feeling a bit guilty about the way her loyalties had been divided, the schoolteacher asked for Mr Nincom's office.

There a voice answered, the voice which Miss Withers remembered as belonging to the small, mousey Smythe person who had reported the story conference in Mr Nincom's office. "Oh, Miss Withers! We've been trying to get in touch with you for hours! You were supposed to ride up to Arrowhead with the rest of the Nincom writers for a story conference this evening. The courier car left at five-thirty. But there'll be another one at ten o'clock in the morning."

Miss Withers was quickly apologetic.

"It doesn't really matter," was the answer, "because Mr Nincom said over the phone that he wanted you especially tomorrow morning. He wants your opinion on a location set that he thinks might do for the Borden place. M.G.M. left a village standing, the one they built for *Of Human Hearts*, and Mr Nincom is thinking of taking it over and using it for *Fall River*."

"I could take a train tonight," the schoolteacher offered. "Or hire a car?"

"That will not be necessary. Anyway, there aren't any trains to Lake Arrowhead. Just be at the studio gate at ten tomorrow morning. You'll see Danny—he's the good-looking driver—in a big Buick sedan with 'Mammoth 17' on the door. And please be on time, because the courier is taking up Mr Nincom's mail, and he can't wait for you."

Miss Withers promised. The duties of a technical expert seemed to extend to a great many things. In comparison with the problem which plagued her the ancient Borden case seemed extremely cold potatoes. But it seemed that whether she wished or not she was going to leave town.

She went up to her room and began hastily to pack. But before she could gather her things together a bellboy arrived with a telegram from New York.

"CONGRATULATIONS HILDEGARDE," said the Inspector, when decoded. "YOU SEEM TO HAVE WALKED INTO A NEST OF TROUBLE. SHALL I COME OUT WITH EXTRADITION PAPERS AND ARREST HIM FOR YOU?"

That was just like Oscar Piper, she thought. He would sit there in his smug little office in Centre Street with its windows looking out on a bare brick wall and its shelves filled with grim "Exhibit As" from old murder cases and send a wire like that.

She wired back.

DON'T BOTHER, HAVE SITUATION WELL IN HAND.
LEAVING FOR ARROWHEAD ON STUDIO BUSINESS IN
MORNING AND WHEN I RETURN EXPECT TO LAY
CASE IN HANDS OF LOCAL POLICE. ALREADY HAVE
FULL DESCRIPTION OF LAVAL AND HAVE MOVED
NEXT DOOR TO HIM. CASE PRACTICALLY CLOSED.
LETTER FOLLOWS. HILDEGARDE.

All except just who and where Derek Laval was and
how he had managed to break a man's neck without a trace
or a sound. But she could fill those blanks in later.

She moved into her new home on Cowbell Canyon
Drive, a street filled now with the harsh rustle of the wind
in the tops of the palms, and wasted no time at all in
unpacking or rearranging. Derek Laval's apartment was in
the other wing of the building, but she hurried there at
once. It was dark and presumably deserted. The schoolteacher tried her own key and found it useless. She tried a
hairpin, and the lock was unpickable. She looked carefully
above the doorjamb and under the mat and in every other
conceivable spot where a key might be hidden, but none
was there.

There was always the rear. Perhaps it would be possible to step from one porch to another, to force a kitchen
window.

That also was a blank wall, and finally even Miss
Withers was forced to give up her attempts at burglary for
the nonce. The lair of Mr Derek Laval was impregnable
unless she used blasting powder or a crowbar.

She was reluctant to call it a day, but there was
nothing else for it. Perhaps, the schoolteacher hoped
wistfully, she would get a suggestion from her subconscious during the night, perhaps she would dream up an
answer to the entire riddle of who and how and why. . . .

Unfortunately her subconscious suggested nothing of
the kind at all, but when she woke in the bright white
California sunshine she realized how, even now, she might

perhaps be able to get inside that apartment and do a bit of concentrated snooping. It was late, nearly nine o'clock in fact, but she still had time. If the plan worked.

She tucked up her hair in an intentionally slovenly fashion, slipped into a morning dress of the accidental type and went out of the apartment house. Around the corner was a tiny grocery store—"market" she must learn to call them out here—and she purchased a bottle of milk, some rolls and oranges. Then she hurried back, rang the door of the manager's apartment.

"So sorry to trouble you," she began breathlessly. "But I'm locked out of my apartment, and the key's inside in my handbag. . . . ."

Mrs Dermott was a plump, tired-looking woman with tiny feet and ankles. The schoolteacher was counting on that, hoping that she would avoid any extra steps. "If you have a master key," Miss Withers suggested brightly, "I'll run right back with it."

It worked. Mrs Dermott produced a small key affixed to a large slab of wood. And Miss Hildegarde Withers did run right back with it, but in the two minutes' interim she opened the door of the Laval apartment and released the lock. So far so good.

She got rid of her unwanted groceries and then calmly marched down the hall and into the apartment which, she confidently expected, would be the end of the trail. And it very nearly was.

For the first few minutes all went well. True, it was difficult to get much of an idea of the character and personality of Mr Laval from this furnished apartment. But there were numerous little things, clues which pointed the way. Or several different ways, it seemed to her.

The living room had been "straightened" without being thoroughly cleaned. Ash trays had been dumped out into the wastepaper basket and set back on the table without being wiped. A glass with half an inch of faintly sour-smelling liquid in it stood beside the couch. There was a small radio, its dial turned to an all-night station.

The wastebasket showed dozens of cigarette stubs, more than half of them lipstick smeared. The brands included four American, two English pure Virginia and one Turkish. The lipstick colors varied from a deep purple to a violent orange. Another glass, broken, was in the wastebasket.

There was a dollar and twenty-one cents in small change down behind the cushions of the divan, as well as two packets of matches with "Swing Club" on the covers, a silver pocket lighter, five blond, one red and two brown hairpins and a lady's vanity case containing Rachel powder and a smashed mirror.

The case would have already been solved by Mr Sherlock Holmes, Miss Withers felt. From the data on hand he could give a minute description of Derek Laval, including his past from the age of six, his taste in food and literature and the color of his eyes.

Unfortunately, the image she was trying to build in her mind steadfastly refused to take shape. The straw man stubbornly refused to be anything else.

She tried the bedroom. One of the twin beds had been made hastily by a man. The other was immaculate. The bedside table contained three packs of cigarettes of three different brands and paper matches advertising half the bars and night spots of the town. There was a telephone on the floor but it was dead. Presumably cut off at the main exchange, she decided. The closet was empty.

The bath produced little more. There were towels, somewhat used. The medicine cabinet showed a cheap electric shaver, a twisted tube of tooth paste and a brush, a packet of razor blades and a tired-looking comb. A safety razor, unassembled, lay on the window sill.

The kitchenette remained. It was evident at once that no food was ever prepared here. The dishes in the cabinet showed a film of dust which was at least six weeks old, and the electric refrigerator held only two bottles of beer, a bottle of White Rock and a lemon.

Beneath the sink reposed several empty soda siphons,

a dozen or so beer bottles and "dead soldiers" galore. Scotch, bourbon, gin, rum.

Mr Laval certainly had catholic tastes in liquors as well as in cigarettes. And in his lady friends, judging by the shades of lipstick, powder and hairpins.

More puzzled than ever, Miss Hildegarde Withers returned to the living room, still doggedly determined to find something which would put her on the right track. There were two closets in this room and they represented the last hope.

The smaller one by the door held a man's hat, a green affair with a rakish Tyrolean feather. It was size 6¾. That was all.

She hurried across the room, realizing that it was late and that she must get out of here in a few minutes if she expected to make the studio by ten o'clock. She tugged at the double doors of the last closet.

There was resistance. For a moment it seemed that someone inside was holding the doors closed or that they were sticking out of pure meanness in an attempt to hinder her. She gave a heavier yank. And then the doors opened, too suddenly.

Skyrockets and Roman candles went off in her head, pinwheels spun in widening circles of red fire. "Earthquake!" Miss Withers thought just before the lights all went out.

V

I know death hath ten thousand several doors
FOR MEN TO TAKE THEIR EXITS; *and 'tis found*
They go on such strange geometrical hinges,
You may open them both ways....

JOHN WEBSTER

"Here comes the cat that ate the canary!" Lillian Gissing said.

Gertrude looked up, saw Jill Madison pushing between the tables, carrying a heavily loaded plate and wearing a soft smile. "She doesn't look like a girl who just lost a fortune, does she?"

"She looks like a gal who just stole my writer," Lillian came back. "I hope it makes her happy."

Jill did look happy. She was happy all by herself in the Mammoth commissary, which is in itself something. For that vast and murky tomb, chilled by the icy blasts of its air-conditioning plant and decorated by sub-W.P.A. murals across its long and windowless walls, would seemingly put a damper on any blithe young heart. But not Jill's. She came on, looking for a place to sit.

Even when four or five companies are working at Mammoth, and during the furious rush of the noon hour, there is usually a table or two vacant in the farthest corner from the door. The folk of Hollywood like to see and be seen, but today swarms of dress extras had been forced to alight even in this outlying nook, and for a moment it appeared that Jill would have to eat her lunch standing up.

Then Gertrude waved at her, indicating the empty chair opposite. "Put it there," she invited inelegantly. Jill hesitated, then sat down.

"I don't see how you get away with it," Lillian greeted her, looking enviously at the loaded plate of smoked Virginia ham and avocados and then at the remains of her own cottage cheese and pineapple salad. "But then, you get away with everything."

"Listen," Jill began hotly. "I didn't——"

"Of course you didn't. Mr Dobie had that cablegram sent to you. He was the cause of your getting the boot, so he took pity on you. What else could he do? Besides, it will make a good story for the gossip columns." Lillian shrugged. "I don't mind if Virgil Dobie wants to make noble gestures. I'm assigned to another writer, anyway, so it's no skin off me."

"She's working for Mr Josef, as of this morning," Gertrude explained.

"Typing out his collection of limericks?" Jill asked.

"Well, after a year of Dobie and Stafford, I guess limericks will be easy. Wait until you find itching powder on your typewriter keys and maybe have your hat blown off by explosive caps shoved into your cigarette ends and——" Lillian stopped short. "And that wasn't half what the 'Katzenjammer Kids' were always doing to me. All the rest of my life I'll have to worry every time I sit down for fear there's a bent pin or a poop cushion in my chair. Or no chair at all!"

"Never a dull moment," Gertrude interposed.

"I think you've all got Mr Dobie wrong," Jill said seriously. "I used to feel about him, about the both of them, just the way you girls do. But if you'll stop and think it was Saul Stafford who thought up most of the gags.

And it was usually Virgil Dobie who tried to square it up afterwards."

"So what? You can't unslap a man's face," Gertrude said. "I'll never get over what happened when Frankie Firsk got married and went on his honeymoon last year. They went to Sun Valley, and the first day a telegram comes calling him back to the studio. So back the newly-weds come to find it was a gag. And they didn't have money enough to go anywhere else, so they spent their honeymoon here in town, watching it rain for two weeks."

"Anyway," Jill cut in, "Dobie and Stafford have made a lot of people laugh. And they've kept this town from taking itself seriously. Mr Dobie says——"

"Whoa!" Gertrude leaned forward. "Rule one. Do not fall in love with boss. Underline. Exclamation point."

Jill blinked. "Oh, don't ever worry about my doing that!" But she stared thoughtfully at a forkful of ham and then put it down as if it appeared very new and strange to her.

"Of course, he's got a wonderful sense of humor—and a wonderful income," Lillian went on. "A girl could do worse. Only Virgil Dobie doesn't go around whistling the 'Wedding March.' Not him. He——"

"For heaven's sake, can't you talk about anything else?" Jill demanded, flushing.

Lillian picked up her luncheon check and rose to her feet. "Sure I can. And one of these days I'm going to talk to Mr Virgil Dobie in a language that he can understand." And she marched off.

Gertrude looked thoughtfully after her. "A venomous bitch," she observed. "I think she's worse since Mr Stafford died. Maybe we're all a little jittery. Not that I think it was anything but an accident, only——"

"Buster says that Miss Withers has proof it was murder!" Jill put in. "He says that she knows the name of the murderer."

"Really?" Gertrude smiled. "When did he tell you all this? I thought you had broken up with Joe College."

"I let him take me to the movies last night," Jill admitted. "But it's the last time. It's just as easy to fall in love with somebody who *has* something. There is no percentage in going around with a nice kid like that—he's so terribly young."

"He's all of your age," Gertrude told her.

Jill smiled wearily to indicate that she was very old and wise. "Besides," she added, "he always wants to take me expensive places, and I can't help realizing all the time that the check is most of his week's salary."

"I wish I had trouble like that," Gertrude told her. "They always want to take me to the beach and *me* to bring the weenies." She looked at her watch. "Almost one-thirty. Time I was getting back to the switchboard. By the way, you said Miss Withers knows the name of the murderer?"

Jill nodded.

"You didn't happen to hear who?"

Jill shook her head. "I guess the old girl is imagining things."

Gertrude rose. "Hope so. Well, enjoy your lunch. By the look of things, you won't have to finish it alone." She nodded toward where Buster Haight was approaching at a dogged trot.

Jill frowned and assumed a properly discouraging attitude. But the young man passed by her with barely the flicker of an eyelash, hurrying on to a table against the wall where Mr Sam Lothian was ministering to his stomach ulcers with milk and crackers. Buster whispered to him for a moment.

Then Mr Lothian pushed back his chair and rose, looking so calm that Jill knew at once something serious had happened. He went out of the commissary.

Jill's smile was almost welcoming as Buster came back along the aisle. "Hi," she greeted him. "What's up—another murder?"

"Huh? Oh, nothing like that." Buster bent down and

spoke softly in her ear. "It's just that Miss Hildegarde Withers has disappeared."

"What?"

He nodded. "She was supposed to arrive up at Arrowhead for a conference with Mr Nincom. But she's disappeared into thin air, and so has the studio car and driver!" Buster cocked his young head sideways. "What's the matter?"

"Just a tiny chill," Jill admitted. "As if—as if somebody were walking over my grave."

Lake Arrowhead, a fresh and lovely blue mirror, hangs high in the mountains above San Bernardino, reflecting white, fleecy clouds, tall pine trees and the French provincial château which Mr Thorwald L. Nincom built three years ago as a refuge from Hollywood. Once built, Mr Nincom discovered that his house was too close to the water and the merry putt-putt of motorboats, so he had it soundproofed. Likewise, the scent of pine trees reminded him unpleasantly of a throat spray he had once been forced to use, so he sealed the windows and installed an air-conditioning plant. The last remaining step was to install a swimming pool which could be heated to tepidity, and then—with the large projection room and a twice-daily courier from the studio—Mr Nincom felt that he was away from it all.

At the moment we find him in the projection room, sitting in utter blackness on a deeply upholstered leather chair and staring at the white screen. Beside him his corps of writers sit and fidget, and, in the row behind, a stenographer waits with poised pencil.

They were watching an old gentleman in side whiskers who snored on a haircloth sofa, with his shoes on the floor beside him. Then Miss Priscilla Lane slunk into the room, holding a hatchet upraised. As she bent over the old gentleman the camera swung toward the window where a curtain bellied outward as if to show the passing of a rather tangible soul.

The screen went black, and then the lights came on. "Well?" demanded Mr Nincom.

"She was swell in the love scenes," said Frankie Firsk politically.

"I don't like the hatchet," quavered Melicent Manning, adjusting her brooch. "It makes me think of red Indians and scalping."

"The real Lizzie Borden used a hatchet, just the same," Mr Nincom said. "Willy, what do you think?"

Willy Abend put out his cigarette. "They're all good tests," he began. "Bari was the best. She makes you feel something of the turmoil, the conflict, that must have been in Lizzie's heart. Gaynor was good too. As a playwright I feel that you should always cast a murderer as unheavy as you can so that the audience won't guess ahead of you."

"Why not Pitts for the part then?" suggested Doug August with a wicked glint in his eye.

Mr Nincom took it seriously. "We tried that once—gave her a sympathetic mother part. The audience laughed at the preview, and we had to reshoot half the picture. She's too typed." He stood up. "No, there'll have to be some more tests taken. In the meantime you can all go back to the scenes you're on. I'm going to spend the afternoon looking at locations if that technical adviser of ours ever gets here." He picked up the phone on the control desk. "Hello? Any word of the courier car yet? What? WHAT? Of course I'll talk to the sheriff's office. Get 'em. . . ."

He hung on for a moment, waiting. "Yes, this is Mr Nincom. Yes. Yes. What? Say it again." His mouth dropped open, and he listened in silence for a long moment. Then he hung up.

"Amazing!" breathed Mr Nincom. "They just found the courier car—at the bottom of Lost Lizard Canyon, six hundred feet beneath the highway!"

The writers surged forward. "And—and the people in

the car?" asked Frankie Firsk. "Miss Withers—and the driver?"

Nincom shook his head. "The sheriff said they were trying to get them out now, but it's an awful job. Ambulances are coming from San Bernardino. As for my mail and my test film, everything is scattered to hell and gone." Mr Nincom pouted. "Everything," he told them, "happens to me!"

For a moment nobody spoke. Then Melicent Manning shivered and said, "Another accident."

"They usually go in threes, don't they? Like deaths among famous people?" Frankie Firsk bit savagely at his forefinger.

Doug August said, "We're all thinking the same thing. Why did it happen to *her?*"

It took a long time to get down into the canyon and up again with the stretchers. And when it was done the intern beside the ambulance refused to do anything about it. "*He's* dead as a duck," said the doctor. "Sawed his throat when he went through the window of the car. And she won't last much longer. I'm not going to have a 'Died in Ambulance' chalked up against me."

Sheriff Truesdale said: "You better take the woman."

"I've already given what first aid I can. It's mostly a matter of minutes."

"Take her," repeated the sheriff. He was a big, soft man with hot, hard eyes that blazed easily. "Get going." He waved his hand. "You never know. She lived this long, didn't she?"

The victims were carted away. A county officer took a picture of the skid marks. "Looks like the road turned, and the car didn't," was his verdict. "No sign of any collision or anything. Unless somebody was coming around the turn on the inside, and they'd have probably stopped."

Sheriff Truesdale nodded. "It could happen. Seems like it would happen at night though. Have somebody put a flare against that busted guardrail." He started toward his car.

"About that wreck down there," a uniformed trooper wanted to know, "do we do anything about it?"

"It belongs to that picture studio. Let them get it. If they can. For all of me, it can stay at the bottom of the canyon." Sheriff Truesdale spat his tobacco over the rim, watching it splatter downward toward the bottom of Lost Lizard Canyon. Then he climbed wearily into his car and drove off after the ambulance, his siren screaming bloody murder.

There wasn't much in the papers next morning. The *Times* said: "ANOTHER FATALITY ON ARROWHEAD ROAD," and the *Examiner:* "ONE DEAD, ONE HURT IN SPECTACULAR PLUNGE," and printed a neat and wholly imaginative drawing showing the studio car hurtling over the edge with a man and woman floating downwards beside it.

"Miss Withers' condition is very critical," spoke the crisp feminine voice of San Bernardino Hospital into the long-distance telephone. "There are multiple fractures of pelvis and both legs, concussion, trauma and serious internal injuries."

"Apart from that, your client is in fine shape," Mr Lothian reported to Harry Wagman. "The studio, of course, is doing everything that can be done. Our insurance policies cover us rather thoroughly in the matter."

At least Mr Lothian hoped that they did.

"Funny, it'd happen to *her*," Wagman said.

"Daniels has been one of our drivers for two years, a very capable young man. Never showed up tight or anything. He was supposed to be a pushover for a cute girl, but I don't suppose he was driving with one hand in this instance."

Harry Wagman didn't smile. "No, I don't guess so. You know, Mr Lothian, it's funny about Miss Withers happening into that thing the other day and then this right on top of it."

"Some people are always getting into jams. The woman is a troublemaker anyway. Have you notified her family?"

If Miss Withers had a family, Wagman indicated, he was completely in the dark about it. "She blew out of her hotel last night, and nobody knows where she moved to. So I can't dig into her luggage."

Mr Lothian frowned. "She's from New York City, isn't she?"

"BUREAU IDENTIFICATION NYC POLICE CENTRE STREET" the message came in over the teletype. "REQUEST AID IN LOCATING RELATIVES OF HILDEGARDE MARTHA WITHERS AGE APPROX FORTY FIVE WHITE AMERICAN SAID TO BE NEW YORKER INJURED SERIOUSLY HERE TODAY COMMUNICATE SAN BERNARDINO SHERIFF'S OFFICE."

The sergeant at Centre Street glanced at the communication, yawned mightily and stuck it on a spindle. He started back to his can of coffee, raised it to his lips and then set it hastily down. "Withers," he muttered. "*Withers . . . !*"

He tore the message off the spindle and ran down the hall toward the Homicide Bureau.

"I thought this might interest you, Inspector, on account of——"

Inspector Oscar Piper had spent the day in court. Now he leaned back in his swivel chair, his brogans on the desk and fat blue smoke rings rising steadily from his pursed lips.

"Tomorrow, Sergeant."

"Yes sir. Only——"

"Tomorrow is another day. Write that in your manual and look at it when your feet hurt." Piper sighed a deep, philosophical sigh.

The sergeant nodded and laid the teletype message on the desk. Then he started to withdraw. There was a thundering crash behind him, and he turned to see the inspector kicking his chair aside, a strangely grim inspector.

"He didn't look as much shocked, exactly, as he looked mad," the sergeant confided to one of the boys in the wardroom later. "For the next five minutes he had everybody going nuts getting him a plane reservation and cashing checks. And then he jumps into a squad car and goes hell-bent for Newark Airport."

"You mean he went to California without any baggage?"

"All the baggage he took with him," admitted the sergeant, "was a bench warrant charging homicide for some guy named Derek Laval."

Next morning the "Rambling Reporter" column in the *Hollywood Reporter* announced:

> "It seems that there's an amusing sequel to the recent rumpus in the Nincom unit at Mammoth. As the result of a gag pulled by Dobie and the late Saul Stafford, both former Nincom writers, the most beauteous blond secretary in the unit got delusions of grandeur and razz-berried herself right out of a job. Virgil Dobie learned this and squared things by putting her back on his own personal pay roll, which so touched and amused Mr Thorwald L. Nincom that he is insisting that Dobie, secretary and all, be reassigned to Nincom Productions' new superspecial. It's a ring-around-a-rosy, and everybody is happy."

In the *Times* Jimmie Fidler wrote: "Memo to staff: Find out if Mammoth is riding for a fall. They've lost two writers by falls this week."

The inspector was unable to read these or any other news notes, being deep in a study of the meager file on the Emily Harris case and somewhat plane-sick besides. He couldn't sleep at all.

"Not that I'm worried about Hildegarde," he kept telling himself. "She's got into some roaring muddle but she'll be all right. She wasn't born to be smashed up in an auto—not her!"

She had probably got too close to the trail of this Laval fellow, and he'd made a desperate attempt to silence her forever. The inspector thought back over the various cases he knew in which the automobile had been used as an intentional instrument of death.

The Torrio mob used to put about three sticks of high-test dynamite under the floor boards of a car, wire it to the ignition and wait for the owner to turn the switch. That was old stuff in the East, but hadn't there been something about a grand-jury investigator named Clinton out there in California? But the bomb-in-car gag didn't fit in exactly. Of course, a good driver—or one in desperation—could force another car off the road. And perhaps off the cliff to hurtle down.

There were tricks that could be pulled with tires, too—and with the exhaust so that the driver of a completely closed car would pass peacefully off to sleep from too much carbon monoxide.

Hildegarde herself, the inspector decided, would be able to put her finger on the probable manner in which it had been accomplished. If she were conscious and able to talk. He smiled at that. Hildegarde would be able to talk, conscious or not.

The big transport plane slipped along westward into the early-morning sunlight at Albuquerque, over the endless frozen waves of the desert. More mountains, more desert, and then they were above the metallic, glossy green of orange groves, slanting down to the coastal plane of southern California.

It was a day among days, the sort of weather that Californians love to call climate. A cloudless sky of soft blue hung over Burbank Airport, and the glow of the sun made the inspector wish he had left his topcoat back in Manhattan along with his toothbrush.

The weather was a good omen, thought Oscar Piper. Nobody could get bad news on a morning like this. His spirits were undampened even when he discovered that the plane had flown him almost straight over San Bernardino and that now he had a good two-hour drive back to the eastward.

There was a cheerful young man with a car for hire at the airport, and the lights were with them all the way out on Foothill Boulevard. And then finally they were in sleepy little San Bernardino; they were pulling up outside the flat little white hospital on the far edge of town. To the north hung a mountain, scarred with a great pale arrowhead, but the inspector had no eye at the moment for scenic beauty.

He walked up the sidewalk toward the hospital door with his fingers crossed. At the steps he paused, studying the green lawn intently, and then pounced. Inspector Oscar Piper had found a four-leafed clover in the grass, a symbol of good luck everywhere but a thousand times more so here and at this time. It was as good as a true shamrock, at least.

Piper stuck it in his lapel and then went inside. At the desk a starched little nurse sat prissily reading the afternoon paper from Los Angeles. "I want to inquire about an accident case you have here," he said. "A Miss Hildegarde Withers?"

"Miss Withers?" repeated the girl.

"Yes!" He nodded. "I've come a long way and I haven't got all day to——"

"Member of the family?"

"No. I mean yes. Why——?"

"Her father?" pressed the nurse.

"Father?" he repeated wonderingly. "No, it's just that I need a night's sleep and a shave. Come on, where is she?"

"She isn't here," he was told.

"Discharged already, huh?" The inspector took a deep sigh for himself.

But the nurse was shaking her head. "I'm sorry, but there was no hope for her from the first. Miss Withers died this morning about six."

The inspector just stood there, not even breathing.

"Everything that could be done for her was done," the nurse continued. "I have her bill right here."

The inspector took it, stared at it as if the long column of figures were Chinese. Automatically he reached for a checkbook.

As he started to scribble the check the girl went on: "The moving-picture studio she worked for sent an ambulance to take the body back to Los Angeles. You must have passed it on the way over. I'm sorry, Mr Laval."

That snapped Oscar Piper out of it as nothing else in the world could have done. "Say that again!" he challenged her.

"I said that I was sorry it turned out——"

"No, the name!"

"Laval? Aren't you him? Because he was calling long distance every hour or so yesterday to ask about Miss Withers. And I thought——"

"Derek Laval, was that the name?"

She nodded, then began to look worried. "Hadn't you better sit down? Would you like a glass of water?"

The inspector flashed his gold badge, and his questions suddenly became crisp and official, impersonal as a robot's. "Did Mr Laval leave a number where you could call him back?"

The girl shook her head.

"Did Miss Withers make any statement before she died?"

"She didn't recover consciousness at any time."

"Do you happen to know where the automobile accident took place?" She told him.

As Inspector Oscar Piper came down the steps of the hospital he saw that a gray bank of fog was drifting over the sky from the west. He walked back to his hired car, his fingers twisting the four-leafed clover into a green pulp.

The driver stared at him. "Say, you better have a drink before we start back to Los Angeles!"

The inspector climbed in. "We're not going back to Los Angeles. Do you know the mountain road to Lake Arrowhead?"

"Sure I do."

"Then get going—and go slow." He leaned back in his seat, realizing that if Miss Hildegarde Withers had been sitting beside him she would have corrected his grammar. "Slowly," he said under his breath.

The car turned right and swung up toward the mountain. "Don't you worry about my going slow on this road," the driver opened up cheerfully. "You can't drive it any other way because of the curves. Why, only the other day there was an accident up here."

"*Was* there?" said the inspector through set teeth.

VI

If the red slayer think he slays
Or if the slain think he is slain,
They know not well **THE SUBTLE WAYS**
I KEEP, *and pass, and turn again.*

RALPH WALDO EMERSON

Mr Nincom was in the groove. After three days of story conference, broken only by the hours of sleep, he had worried and fretted his corps of writers to the point where he was almost certain to get something spectacular out of them. He worked on the oyster plan—irritate enough and you may get a pearl.

He had them all grouped in the long living room of his mountain hideaway amid dozens of leering animal heads, stuffed and painted sailfish and similar trophies of the hill and the deep. Ash trays were heaping full, pencils were stubby and there wasn't a decent fingernail in the entire squad.

Nincom marched up and down before the ten-foot fireplace, one hand clutching his little rosewood baton. He stopped, aimed it at nothing.

"I'm not satisfied with the setup, not satisfied at all," he told them. "This has got to be a *big* picture. Now what"—and he aimed at Melicent Manning—"what does it need to make it *big?*"

83

"It's the theme that's weak," she ventured nervously. "We've got a wonderful love story between Lizzie and the lawyer. But it comes to nothing. If we could take out the murders and build up the love..."

Nincom turned to Frankie Firsk. "What do you think of that?"

Firsk hesitated, trying vainly to get a clue to what the great man was thinking. "It's not a bad idea," he ventured. "Maybe Lizzie *didn't* kill her father and her stepmother. Maybe the stepmother killed the father and then committed suicide. And Lizzie wanted to keep the family name clear and she..."

"Sewage," interrupted Mr Nincom.

"Take out the love story," suggested Doug August. "Build up the murders. Make it a story of hate. Lizzie murders three or four other people. Townspeople fear her but they're afraid to talk. A sort of 'M' character."

"I'm having trouble enough casting Lizzie without trying to find a she-Peter Lorre," Nincom said. "Mr Abend, does your vast experience on the Hungarian stage inspire you to any bright ideas?"

"Brotherhood—that's the keynote to strike. We can get some social significance in the picture. Lizzie is furious at her father for the way his captains treat the crews of the family whaling ships. She is a direct descendant of Barbara Frietchie, and Lizzie treasures the American flag that old Frietchie designed. She's a hotheaded idealist, see? This builds up into a family quarrel, and Lizzie strikes a blow in anger. Not for herself, but for the exploited mariners...."

"More sewage," decided Mr Nincom. "Besides, it was Betsy Ross. Anyway, we're selling entertainment, not waving flags. Leave that to Warner Brothers; they discovered patriotism." He turned to Virgil Dobie who was busily making notes on a sheet of yellow paper. "Well?"

"I haven't been on the story quite as long as the rest of you," Dobie began. "But here's something that occurred to me on my layoff. Everybody loves a mystery. So why not leave it up in the air?—did Lizzie Borden bump off her family or didn't she? At the end leave it to the audience. Is she guilty and fit for hanging or does she go free to marry her lawyer boy friend? The screen goes dark for five minutes while the house lights come on and everybody gives a standing vote. Then the operator flashes the one of the two endings that they've chosen...."

"No! No! No! They've already got their hats on and are hell-bent out of the theater," Mr Nincom objected. "It's a novel idea, but——"

"Novel?" Virgil Dobie laughed. "It's the newest idea since they invented close-ups. I don't see why——" He stopped suddenly and motioned toward the door. "Uncle Remus wants something."

Mr Nincom turned impatiently to face the white-jacketed darky who lurked in the doorway. "I told you we were not to be disturbed for any reason...."

"'Scuse," said Uncle Remus. "Gentleman to see you. I tole him nothin' doin'. He come inside anyway."

"What? Well, tell him——"

"I don' tell the law nothin'," said Uncle Remus definitely. "He got a big gold badge and he's mad." The darky came closer. "It's about that accident the other day."

"Tell him that it's in the hands of the sheriff," Mr Nincom exploded. "He can get everything he needs from Sheriff Truesdale."

"Sheriff brought him," confided Uncle Remus. "This's a really big law man. Sheriff calls him 'Mr.'"

Mr Nincom took this, blinked and then nodded. "I'll try to see them in a moment," he decided. He turned to his writing staff. "This has nothing to do with you, so let's not waste any valuable time. We have a release date to meet, you know. So go to your rooms and tear up everything you've done on 'Sequence D' and start all over. Frankie, you and Douglas see what can be done with Ellis' part. It's got to be built up or Cooper will never accept it——"

"I'm for Melvyn Douglas anyway," Doug August said.

"All right, all right. Virgil, bear down on the comedy

situations, especially in the courtroom. . . . Lizzie's uncle, old Vinnicum Morse—he ought to be worth building up. Maybe we can cast Guy Kibbee. Or Tom Mitchell. And the ladies of the church . . . no, you better make them the Woman's Club to play safe. Anyway, they can be played broader—a sort of Greek chorus of harpies. Remember, all of you, this is a *big* picture. Murder is a *big* theme. Love is a *big* theme. We've got both of them. . . ."

He waved them away, nodded to the secretary who had been hammering away on the noiseless typewriter in the corner. "Take a rest, Caroline," he said kindly. "And while you're resting you can look up those references I gave you. Oh yes, and call up every place in Los Angeles where they might have ship models. Lizzie's home should be full of ship models."

Alone at last, Mr Nincom sat down at his desk and pressed a button, filling the room with the recorded music of a martial band playing the "Finale" from *William Tell*. He conducted this with closed eyes and much flourishing of the little baton. Then, and not until then, the great man signaled that his uninvited guests might enter the Presence.

It was immediately obvious that Uncle Remus had made an understatement when he said that the inspector had a big gold badge and was mad. Oscar Piper was madder than that.

"But why, why do you come to me?" Mr Nincom opened up when he learned the object of the call. "This Withers woman had just started to work in my unit. I know nothing of her except that she seemed to be well recommended. And if she had an accident on the way up here in a studio car it is no affair of mine. Let her heirs bring suit against the studio if they think they have a case. All I know is that the whole thing has inconvenienced me considerably and that——"

"It wasn't an accident," interrupted the inspector. "None of these accidents have been accidents." He chopped off his words as if it hurt him to speak.

"*Not* an accident?" Mr Nincom blinked.

"That's what Inspector Piper seems to think," interrupted the sheriff in a placatory tone. "I know how you feel, Mr Nincom, and how busy you are. But I have an idea that maybe if you could co-operate for a few minutes and maybe answer a couple of questions, why, it would all be straightened out."

Mr Nincom was obviously being very, very patient. "Please go on."

Piper said: "Was it your idea—bringing Miss Withers up here in the mountains?"

"It was not. I often bring my writing staff. But not a technical adviser. I only sent for her because one of the studio executives felt that she was stirring up trouble and it would be a good idea to get her out of town for a few days."

"I see." The inspector made a note or two. "Who knew that she was coming up here?"

"Huh? Why, everybody. Anybody. It was no secret. They were trying to find her all over the studio that afternoon, and I suppose anybody there could have picked up the information."

"Thanks. And this studio car. Where was it kept?"

Mr Nincom was boiling. "My time is worth one thousand dollars an hour—and you keep me here asking silly questions! How should I know where studio cars are kept? In the studio garage, I suppose." He urged them both toward the door. "If there's anything more, gentlemen, I hope you'll go to Mr Lothian or Chief Sansom at the studio. There's nothing more I can tell you, and I have a staff of writers waiting for me."

"Funny you're in such a hurry to get back to them," the inspector told him, "when you figure that it's ten to one that you're nursing a murderer among them."

Nincom froze. "*What?* What are you saying?"

"A quadruple murderer." The inspector stood on the balls of his feet like a marksman taking aim. "Emily Harris back in New York. That was one. Saul Stafford was two.

The driver, Daniels, was three—and Miss Withers four. Four victims."

Mr Nincom looked puzzled and annoyed. "Aren't you jumping to conclusions, Inspector?"

"That's what I been telling him," the sheriff hastily put in. "Things like that don't happen out here. In New York or those places maybe. But not here." He unbuttoned the top button of his trousers and exhaled. "Other cars have gone off into Lost Lizard Canyon. Been several accidents along there."

Nincom nodded. "A dangerous spot in the road. I've noticed it."

"It might be possible to tamper with the mechanism of an automobile," the inspector said, "so that later— perhaps hours later—it would go out of control."

Sheriff Truesdale shook his head. "Sounds kinda complicated to me. I'll believe that when I see it. Now if you had some proof——"

The inspector thought of the envelope in the breast pocket of his rumpled and torn coat and smiled a hard smile.

"I still don't see what I have to do with this," Mr Thorwald L. Nincom announced. "I am naturally sorry to lose one of my employees but I'm afraid that your suspicions, Inspector, sound like some plot that one of my writers might dream up. And, frankly, it's a plot that I would reject instantly. Sheriff Truesdale, I'm surprised that you make yourself a party to——"

"Now, wait a minute," insisted the sheriff. "I may not agree with the inspector. But the law has to stick together."

"Thank you," said the inspector stiffly. "Perhaps you're not aware, Mr Nincom, that if I request it the sheriff here is in duty bound to arrest anyone I point out and hold them in jail while I apply for extradition papers."

"Inspector Piper thinks that maybe one of your writers is the man he's after," the sheriff explained.

"Sewage," cut in Mr Nincom.

"All the same, I have in my pocket a warrant for the

Introducing the first and only complete hardcover collection of Agatha Christie's mysteries

Now you can enjoy the
greatest mysteries ever written
in a magnificent
Home Library Edition.

Discover Agatha Christie's world of mystery, adventure and intrigue

Agatha Christie's timeless tales of mystery and suspense offer something for every reader—mystery fan or not—young and old alike. And now, you can build a complete hardcover library of her world-famous mysteries by subscribing to The Agatha Christie Mystery Collection.

This exciting Collection is your passport to a world where mystery reigns supreme. Volume after volume, you and your family will enjoy mystery reading at its very best.

You'll meet Agatha Christie's world-famous detectives like Hercule Poirot, Jane Marple, and the likeable Tommy and Tuppence Beresford.

In your readings, you'll visit Egypt, Paris, England and other exciting destinations where murder is always on the itinerary. And wherever you travel, you'll become deeply involved in some of the most ingenious and diabolical plots ever invented ... "cliff-hangers" that only Dame Agatha could create!

It all adds up to mystery reading that's so good ... it's almost criminal. And it's yours every month with The Agatha Christie Mystery Collection.

Solve the greatest mysteries of all time. The Collection contains all of Agatha Christie's classic works including *Murder on the Orient Express, Death on the Nile, And Then There Were None, The ABC Murders* and her ever-popular whodunit, *The Murder of Roger Ackroyd.*

Each handsome hardcover volume is Smythe sewn and printed on high quality acid-free paper so it can withstand even the most murderous treatment. Bound in Sussex-blue simulated leather with gold titling, The Agatha Christie Mystery Collection will make a tasteful addition to your living room, or den.

Ride the Orient Express for 10 days without obligation. To introduce you to the Collection, we're inviting you to examine the classic mystery, *Murder on the Orient Express*, without risk or obligation. If you're not completely satisfied, just return it within 10 days and owe nothing.

However, if you're like the millions of other readers who love Agatha Christie's thrilling tales of mystery and suspense, keep *Murder on the Orient Express* and pay just $9.95 plus postage and handling.

You will then automatically receive future volumes once a month as they are published on a fully returnable, 10-day free-examination basis. No minimum purchase is required, and you may cancel your subscription at any time.

This unique collection is not sold in stores. It's available only through this special offer. So don't miss out, begin your subscription now. Just mail this card today.

BUSINESS REPLY MAIL

FIRST CLASS   PERMIT NO. 2154   HICKSVILLE, N.Y.

Postage will be paid by addressee:

The Agatha Christie
Mystery Collection
Bantam Books
P.O. Box 956
Hicksville, N.Y. 11802

arrest of Derek Laval, alias John Doe——" Piper stopped short. "Know him?" For a moment the movie producer had looked very startled.

"Laval?" Mr Nincom nodded slowly. "Yes. I mean no. But somebody by that name sent me an obscene Christmas card last year. It was really——" He shuddered.

Piper went on. "A warrant for arrest on the charge of murder in the borough of Manhattan, city and state of New York. He is a white male known to have resided in Greenwich Village for some time but left there about six years ago. Said to be a writer of free verse. Does that fit any member of your writing staff?"

"It fits them all," Nincom shot back.

Sheriff Truesdale grunted appreciatively, but the inspector did not seem to think it funny. "Meaning what?"

Mr Nincom balanced his toy baton on one forefinger and stared at the ceiling. "Meaning that there isn't a writer in Hollywood who didn't first try his fortune in New York. And ninety per cent of them wrote poetry in the late teens and early twenties. Poetry is a symptom of adolescence in the writer, like pimples and open jallopies and jitterbugging for other youths."

"Thanks," said the inspector. "And that's all the help you can give us?"

Nincom shrugged. "I'm afraid so."

"Too bad," Oscar Piper mused. "This means that the whole thing will have to be dragged out in the newspapers. I was hoping that we could manage with a minimum of publicity."

That shot hit home. "Wait a moment," said Mr Nincom. "If—if it's just a matter of eliminating my staff of writers I might be able to help you. Have you a picture of this Laval?"

The inspector shook his head. "Unfortunately," he admitted, "we are required by law to return photographs and fingerprints to a person when we release them. I didn't handle the case personally, being out of town at the time, so I wouldn't recognize Laval if he were as close to me as you are."

Nincom shrugged. "Then if you have no means of identifying your man . . ."

"But we have. Part of the evidence impounded in the case was a drinking glass known to have been last used by Derek Laval. On it was the smudged print of a right thumb and a clear print of a right finger—which one nobody knows. The glass is broken now. We haven't even the print, just the key number—7 B over 3, it was. That means that Laval—no matter what name he uses now— has a *lateral pocket loop* on one finger of his right hand. It's a fairly unusual formation. So we can instantly eliminate everyone who hasn't such a loop."

Nincom looked both irritated and dubious. He bent his baton nervously until it seemed about to snap. "But, really, Inspector, much as I would like to co-operate with you, I don't see how you can expect to drag my entire staff off to some police station and force them to undergo fingerprinting."

"The inspector don't mean that," put in Sheriff Truesdale. "He ain't asking for trouble."

"I'm not ducking it either. I have personal reasons for cracking this case, no matter whose pink toes get stepped on. There is one way that I think might work so that we could find out whether or not you have a murderer under your wing." The inspector explained what was in his mind.

"As easy as that, eh?" Nincom frowned.

Piper said: "It could be."

"Of course, one doesn't like to feel that there's a homicidal maniac around," Mr Nincom said slowly. "If this works——"

"It can't do any harm," Piper said. "Actually, it's a sort of guessing game—a game with a catch to it."

Nincom wasn't listening. "It's something like the scene I worked out to trap the killer in *Harm's Way*, the picture I directed over at Elstree. That was the year they traded me for Hitchcock. Ah, those were the days!"

"Well?" said the inspector. "Yes or no?"

Thorwald L. Nincom didn't answer. He was pacing up and down the room. "Lights here—and here!" he decided. "I send for the writers—they enter over there. You sit here, Inspector. . . ." He nodded. "It's a very interesting problem in stagecraft."

The writers of the Nincom unit were summoned to appear in the living room at once. Willy Abend was interrupted in the middle of what he hoped would be the lyrics for a new national anthem to replace the unsingable and incendiary strains of "The Star-Spangled Banner." It began: "Out of workers' sweat came America. . . ." He pushed this interesting if extracurricular activity aside and hurried downstairs.

Doug August and Frankie Firsk were reading the third sequence aloud, August taking the lines of Lizzie Borden and Firsk those of her sweetheart lawyer, Ellis. He read in a falsetto voice: "How can you say that?"

The other man took it up. "But I must, Ellis dear. You are to go away and forget me."

"Forget you? Ha ha. How can I ever forget you? Lizzie, you're the most adorable poison that ever got into a man's blood."

"Not so good," Doug August decided, back in his own voice. "That last line——"

"Oughta be '*sweetest* poison,'" interrupted Uncle Remus from the doorway. "Lizzie, you're the sweetest poison what ever got into a man's veins."

They both looked at him and then at each other. "He's right," August decided. "It's not so corny that way."

Frankie Firsk nodded. "If we use it we'll have to give him screen credit."

Uncle Remus laughed. "I don't want no credit. I only want you should come downstairs before Mr Nincom gets into a tantrum. He wants you to have a cocktail with that law man from New York."

The writers blinked.

"Oh, frabjous day!" murmured Frankie Firsk. "We are to be plied with the cup that cheers. . . ."

"Something is up," Doug August decided. "Hey, Uncle. What makes? I mean, what's all the fuss about downstairs?"

Uncle Remus' face took on an expression of outraged propriety. "Beg pardon?"

"What's the matter, couldn't you hear anything through the door?"

Uncle Remus said: "I hear plenty. An' I don' talk. You better hurry on now."

They went on but they did not hurry. In fact, both Firsk and August went down the stairs as if they would rather not.

The colored man went on, knocked on Melicent Manning's door. That lady, deep in the diary which someday she hoped to publish under the title, *Fifty Years a Glamour Girl*, put it well out of sight and hung on another scarf and two bracelets. Then, equipped for anything, she went on downstairs.

That was the list, except for Virgil Dobie who wasn't in his room at all. Uncle Remus finally ran him to earth in Mr Nincom's private study, talking over the open wire to the studio switchboard. Both study and telephone were supposed to be sacred.

"Mr Nincom won't like you to use that line," the colored man interrupted. "That line is for business."

". . . and I don't want to hear when I get back that any office boy has been beating my time. Yes, tomorrow sometime, I think. His Nibs won't make us work all day Sunday. So hold my mail there and keep Monday night open. 'By, now."

"Mr Nincom, he says . . ."

"Okay, Uncle Eight-Ball. It was a business call. Just checking up with my secretary back at the studio."

Uncle Remus looked very doubtful. "You always call your secretary 'Miss Fancypants'?" He shrugged. "Anyway, you're wanted in the living room. Everybody wanted in the living room."

Virgil Dobie raised his high Satanic eyebrows. "Trouble?"

"Could be," Uncle Remus admitted. "For somebody."

It didn't start out like trouble. The kitchen boy brought a big tray of highballs which were passed around. The sheriff knocked his off in a gulp. Mr Nincom sipped at one, and Inspector Oscar Piper put his glass, untasted, on a near-by table.

There was a certain stiffness in the gathering—no one could deny that. Melicent Manning, as the only lady present, tried to make conversation. "As an officer, Inspector, what is your feeling about the Lizzie Borden case? You've heard of it, I presume?"

He nodded. "Juries are more sensible nowadays. Lizzie today would get what Ruth Snyder got—a quick sizzle in the hot squat."

"But a *woman* . . ."

"Women are usually pretty good at murder," Piper said. That slowed up the conversation. Most of the glasses were by this time empty, and Mr Nincom gave a brief signal toward the doorway. At once Uncle Remus entered with a tray and started gathering them up. Nobody seemed to notice that he picked up each glass by the very top and set them on the tray in an orderly circle.

It was Mr Nincom's cue, and he rose to it. "You are probably wondering why I asked you all to come down here," he began. "It is because the inspector here has made a suggestion. He has a slight request to make of you." And Nincom nodded toward his guest.

Oscar Piper stood up. "Thanks." His chill gray eyes moved from one to the other. "It's just this, folks. I have reason to believe that one of you may be the person I have a John Doe warrant for. The sheriff, Mr Nincom and I have agreed that in fairness to the rest of you we ought to do all the eliminating we can. So I want you to give me your fingerprints voluntarily."

The silence in the room was thick as mush.

"Of course, you have the privilege of refusing. That refusal can be taken only one way. So——"

Melicent Manning stood up with a clatter of bracelets. "Of all things! I've never in my life been so grossly insulted! If——"

Things were rapidly getting out of hand. "Wait a minute," put in Sheriff Truesdale sensibly. "The inspector here is looking for a man. So you're really not one of the suspects at all." She sat down, somewhat mollified.

Willy Abend murmured something about "Cossacks." "My fingerprints are my own affair," he insisted. "The Bill of Rights guarantees the freedom and sanctity of the individual. One of the unalienable privileges——"

"Okay." Piper cut him short. "Save the speech." He looked toward Virgil Dobie. "Well?"

"I'm with Willy on that point," Dobie said. "I don't know why, but I've always had a dislike of giving out my fingerprints. I wouldn't even let them put my print on my driver's license when I had it renewed. But I'll give you an autographed copy of the X ray of my arm the time I broke it." The inspector failed to smile.

Frankie Firsk said, "I don't see why I should be the only one. I mean, if everybody else did it I wouldn't mind. But now——"

Douglas August was the only one left. "How about you?" Piper demanded.

August smiled sweetly. "It's a waste of time," he said.

"Why?" snapped Piper.

"Because you've already got our fingerprints. On those highball glasses. You see, Inspector, I've written Mr Moto and Bulldog Drummond into the same situation so many, many times that it's old stuff."

The silence in the room grew very brittle. "So that's why Uncle Remus snatched the glasses!" exploded Virgil Dobie. "Not bad, Inspector. Not bad at all."

Piper nodded. "I confess that I'd hoped that the man I want—and *only* the man I want—would refuse to have prints taken. But thank you all just the same." He nodded at Mr Nincom.

"That will do," said Nincom. "Back to your typewriters."

Puzzled and uneasy, the little conclave of writers started out of the room. Sheriff Truesdale went to the kitchen door and said, "Okay, Uncle. Bring back the glasses."

"Comin'!"

Through the doorway came Uncle Remus, proud and happy, holding the tray of empty glasses high on one palm. His ebony countenance was alight with excitement—and then he tripped over the sill and slid into the room amid a crash of glassware.

Then the startled laughter of the writers came back to mock the unhappy inspector, Frankie Firsk's nervous giggle above the deep boom of Virgil Dobie. The door closed behind them.

"Tough luck," said the sheriff. "Seems like this isn't your day, Inspector."

Piper was talking to himself, fervently and sulphurously. There wasn't a piece of glass on the floor bigger than a dime. Uncle Remus picked himself up but, instead of the apologies one might have expected, he still wore a happy smile.

"Nice work!" congratulated Mr Nincom.

Piper whirled on him. "You told him to do that? Why——"

Nincom nodded. He crossed to the door, made sure that the writers were out of earshot on their way upstairs. Then he came back. "A little touch of my own," he admitted. "There was no use letting any of them think you had their prints. So I had my man stage the spill with some fresh glasses."

"Here's the *real* ones," offered Uncle Remus, re-appearing with a duplicate tray. "They start right here at this end, just like everybody sat. Mr. Firsk and Mr Dobie..."

Inspector Oscar Piper took a deep breath, shook his head and sat down at the table. Mr Nincom and the sheriff watched with deep interest as he borrowed a small brush, a saucer and a candle from Uncle Remus.

"This might make a very good scene in a picture," Nincom decided as he watched the inspector smoke up the saucer, whisk off soot enough to stain the fingerprints. But it was a slow and painstaking job, and Mr Nincom, used to having his results all worked out beforehand, soon began to fidget impatiently. "Well," he demanded finally, "which one is it?"

"Don't know yet," murmured Piper.

Mr Nincom began to stalk up and down. "If I were casting this I think I'd pick Virgil Dobie for the killer. He's the best type in the bunch," he hinted hopefully.

"Murderers in real life look like just anybody else," the inspector said. "Judd Gray was the most harmless-looking little guy you ever met. And Hauptmann—you'd pick him any day for an honest German carpenter." He dabbed soot on another glass, held it up to the light.

"Really!" burst forth Mr Nincom a bit later. "After all, Inspector, I have given you every opportunity. It can't possibly take this long. If for any reason you're playing for time——"

"I'm only beginning," Piper told him.

At that point Mr Thorwald L. Nincom obviously lost all interest in the game. "If you gentlemen will excuse me," he said, "I usually take a siesta before dinner."

He edged himself out of the room. Unimpressed, the inspector fiddled away with brush and powder and glasses while Sheriff Truesdale snored softly in a big easy chair.

Finally Piper pushed away his utensils and mopped his forehead. "Hell's fire!" he said.

The sheriff woke up at once. "No good?" he inquired eagerly.

Piper hesitated. "*Too* good, really. Remember I said that the man I'm looking for had a lateral pocket loop on one finger of his right hand?"

The sheriff nodded. "Uh-huh. And now I s'pose that

you found that every one of the suspects has that kind of a loop, is that it?"

It was a good guess, but the inspector shook his head. There was deep bitterness in his tone. "No, nothing like that. *None* of them has it—except the one person who can't be the man I'm looking for."

Sheriff Truesdale pursed his lips. "You don't mean *him*? It ain't Nincom?"

"The only person in this house with a lateral pocket loop on a finger of the right hand is Melicent Manning, the old lady with the bracelets."

"Say!" breathed the sheriff. "I betcha——"

Piper shook his head. "And don't you leap to the conclusion that she was in New York eight years ago, disguised as a man. Because the guy I'm looking for had a beard, and I doubt if she could manage that. Moreover, this Laval was held a couple of days on suspicion in the precinct station. And I don't think that those boys would miss a masquerade like that. No, it's a blind alley. All you can do when you strike a snag like this is to start all over again. I'm heading back."

"Back to New York?" inquired the sheriff, almost too eagerly.

Piper shook his head. "I'm not going back to New York until and unless I can take a certain guy's scalp with me." He stood up. "I meant back to Los Angeles."

"Sure, I'll drive you as far as San Bernardino," Sheriff Truesdale said.

"I suppose we ought to say something to Mr Nincom," Piper observed. "After all, he did stage the thing for us." He found the bell, rang it and spoke to Uncle Remus.

The darky promised to take a message to his employer. "Mr Nincom's not in his room right now," he said. "But I tell him."

"Tell him it's still up in the air," Piper said. "But I've got a couple of hot leads."

"Sure, I tell him," Uncle Remus said again. He turned to the sheriff. "Your office, they want you to call. I didn't like to disturb you, but maybe you better call back, Sheriff."

Sheriff Truesdale nodded. "You can use that phone right there," Uncle Remus offered.

As he went to make his call the inspector walked slowly out into the chilly air of the early evening. Wisps of fog moved overhead, some of them slipping through the very tops of the trees. Automatically he put a cigar in his mouth and lighted it, finding it dry and bitter, as all cigars had been since the news about Hildegarde had reached him.

Finally the sheriff came out. "Oh, here you are!" he said. "Thought for a minute that I saw you heading down the path toward my car. Say, Inspector, would you mind very much if I didn't give you that lift after all? On account of I have to spend some time here in Arrowhead."

"Crime wave?" Piper asked.

The sheriff smiled. "Nothing that would seem like much back where you come from. It's just a family matter. The cook up at the big hotel thinks that his wife run off with some other guy. I got to do some investigating." Sheriff Truesdale led the way to where his little sedan was parked on Nincom's shaded driveway. "I can drop you off at the bus station, Inspector."

So it happened that Inspector Oscar Piper slept fitfully in the rear of a big Greyhound bus as it wound downwards from Lake Arrowhead that night while the sheriff busied himself with official errands around the little mountain resort. The missing wife thing was a dud, as he had known it would be. Those hotel cooks were always having trouble with their wives. On account of they kept such funny hours. And what woman would want to try to cook for a chef?

Finally Sheriff Truesdale found that the man with whom the missing wife was supposed to have eloped was deep in a stud poker game in the back room at the tavern. "The woman's probably sneaked down to L.A. for a toot," was his final verdict. It wouldn't be the first time.

He might just as well have driven that New York inspector down the mountain, Sheriff Truesdale was thinking. It would have meant pleasant company on the way home, and once in a while a man can pick up something new from those big-city men. Like smoking up a saucer to make soot for fingerprint tests. He swung his little car up the steep grade from the village, swung around through the hotel park, heading for home.

No, not for home. Because at the last sharp turn the steering wheel gave in his hands and then spun foolishly. The road turned, but the sheriff and his little black sedan kept going straight ahead down through the flower gardens and off a sort of steep toboggan slide of underbrush and across a rocky beach into five feet of water. Lake Arrowhead was colder than death.

Sheriff Truesdale climbed out on the roof of his sunken sedan and howled for help like a trapped wolf.

VII

I must become **A BORROWER OF THE NIGHT**
For a dark hour or twain....

WILLIAM SHAKESPEARE

Rain in California is like rain nowhere else in the world. Let it come down for half an hour, and it seems that it has been raining forever and ever. And that it must continue until half-past Eternity.

Over the lovely if artificial landscape, over the bright houses and the round brown-green hills comes a deathly gray pallor, a gloom of low clouds and everlasting chilly downpour. The color seems to seep out of everything, as if the projection machine in a motion-picture theater had suddenly switched from technicolor to ordinary black-and-white film.

And it rains!

In Hollywood Santa Monica Boulevard becomes a river dotted with little islands that are stalled and abandoned cars. Where Eastern elms and maples would toss and dance delightedly in the deluge, the palms drip and shiver in the streets, tall, lonely anachronisms, geological freaks which seem to have been left out by some forgetful florist after a wedding.

The gutters run full, higher than the curbs. And there are few children to run up and down barefoot, screaming and sailing their boats of shingle, for mothers remember the little boy a year or so ago who was washed down into the sewer and out to sea. . . .

So it rained that Sunday, the morning after Inspector Oscar Piper's return by bus from Lake Arrowhead. It rained without wind, without thunder or lightning and without a pause.

Especially fitting weather, the inspector thought, considering the grim errands he had to do. At the little mortuary on Western Avenue he was hard put to it to avoid a salesman for Woodbine Acres who kept pointing out the unequaled charms and attractions of that celebrated burial ground. Piper finally voted against purchasing either a "view lot" close by an everlasting fountain or a cubbyhole in the "Chamber of Eternal Peace" where each niche bore the name of its occupant in letters of solid bronze and where a concealed organ played Brahms twenty-four hours a day, presumably until drowned out by the Last Trump.

Miss Hildegarde Withers, he was certain, would care neither for the everlasting fountain nor the ever-playing organ, so he made preliminary arrangements to ship her mortal remains back to Manhattan.

The undertaker led the conversation gently around to the subject of photographs. "If you had a picture of the departed it would aid our staff of lady morticians in restoring a perfect likeness. The accident, you know . . ."

Piper said there was no portrait available and got out of there as quickly as possible. But not quite quickly enough. As he came out of the place a brawny man fell into step beside him, shouldered him expertly back into a comparatively dry doorway. It was a flat-footed technique that the inspector recognized.

"All right, bud," said the man in a heartily unpleasant tone. "Why all the interest in that stiff in there?"

The inspector considered for a moment. He was in a mood to throw a punch. This flat-footed moron would be a sucker for a left, especially if you stood on his foot when you threw it. On the other hand, he was presumably doing his duty.

"Will you take a ride down to headquarters or talk here and now?"

"Relax," said the inspector. "Show your authority if you have any."

"Tom Sansom, special officer," he was told. A badge was flashed.

Piper grinned and showed his own. "I've heard of you," he said. "You're the one who jumped on the thumbtack." Sansom suddenly looked like a dog who has been playing a game with a balloon and has had it pop in his face.

"Why are *you* so interested in what's inside there?" Piper demanded. "I thought all you local masterminds had decided it was an accident?"

"Sorry, Inspector," Sansom said. "But after I heard from Sheriff Truesdale up at Arrowhead this morning I began to wonder. So I put a man on the mortuary here. . . ."

"Truesdale? But he didn't think that I was on the right track," Piper began.

"He does now. After what happened to him last night. His steering gear went haywire, and he got dunked in Lake Arrowhead. The sheriff thinks it was meant for you and him both. If he'd driven you down the mountain as he planned to do——" Sansom shrugged.

"Yeah, I see. That might convince even the sheriff."

"Myself, I'm not convinced," Sansom said. "I think it's all phony. Sounds like one of the 'B' thrillers our studio writers turn out in two weeks. But it's my job to leave no stone unturned. . . ."

"Save the speech. It's murder all right. I'm out here to do what I can. Do we co-operate or not?"

Sansom hesitated. "Look here, we know our business. The coroner said——"

"Coroners can make mistakes. Hildegarde Withers was killed because she was too close to the murderer. It was an accident on purpose. Do you know a man named Derek Laval, sometimes known as Dick Laval?"

"I've heard the name," the studio cop admitted. "Don't know as I've ever met him."

"I'm going to meet him. And when I do——" Piper's hand clenched into a fist. "Miss Withers sent me several letters and telegrams. Not much to go on, but enough so I know she was close on Laval's trail. She figured that he was using another name, a sort of nom de plume in the studio."

Sansom considered that. "What are you going to do about it, Inspector?"

"I'll figure out something. First of all, I want to find out where Miss Withers was living. She checked out of her hotel Wednesday and didn't leave an address. Has the studio got the new one?"

"No. All the address we have is just the Roosevelt. We tried to find out where she'd gone and didn't get to first base." Sansom took off his hat, shook the water from the brim. "Funny she didn't put her address on the letters she wrote to you."

"She did. The studio address. Which puts us right back where we were." The inspector frowned. "Of course, there's always the chance that she wrote me a letter that didn't arrive at Centre Street until after I left night before last. She might have put the new address on that."

"What do you figure on finding in her apartment?"

"Don't know," Piper admitted. "Maybe some notes on the case. Maybe something that points in the direction she was moving." He nodded. "I've got a notion to call my office in New York and see if anything's come in. Care to wait around?"

Sansom looked at him oddly. "Sure," he said. "I'd like to watch how you big-town fellows work. Pick up some hints maybe." The inspector saw only a blandly innocent face but he had an idea that this man and he would never become bosom friends.

All the same, they climbed into Sansom's car and

splashed through the streets to the hotel. The studio officer sat on the edge of the bed while Piper put through a long-distance call to Centre Street. There would be a crew, a very slim skeleton crew, on duty at Homicide on a Sunday afternoon.

Finally the inspector heard the familiar voice of Lieutenant Georgie Swarthout. "Oh, hello," said that worthy young officer. "How'd you find our friend Miss Withers?"

"Never mind," Piper snapped. "Georgie, go up to my desk and see if there is any mail. I mean letters from out here in California. I'll hold on."

The minutes ticked away, and Piper had an unjust suspicion that Swarthout was looking through his desk to see if he kept any cigars about. Then the line clicked. "No, no letters," was the report. "But there's a big brown envelope with a California postmark that came in yesterday. It's marked 'Fragile and Personal.'"

That sounded very much like Hildegarde's work. "Open it," Piper said. He looked over his shoulder and saw that Officer Sansom was trying very hard to read one of Miss Withers' old telegrams upside down. "Don't strain your eyes," he said to the man over his shoulder. "Go on, help yourself!"

Officer Sansom, unabashed, picked up the message, puzzling over the first word. "'JSBR MPY . . .'" he tried to pronounce. "Oh, *code!*"

"It means 'have not,'" Piper told him. Over the excellent connections of the Bell and Associated telephone companies of America he heard clearly the sound of tearing paper three thousand miles away and then Lieutenant Swarthout's voice. "Say, here *is* something, Inspector!"

"Yeah?"

"I don't just know what. Looks like photographs. Yes, seven photographs. Something out of the family album. They all have been decorated up. Looks like that guy who draws mustaches on the pretty-girl posters in the subway has been working here. Each of the guys in the photos has

a false beard drawn on his phiz. No—correction. One of
'em really has a beard. The rest——"

"Okay. Is there a note of anything?"

"Nope. Oh yes, there is too. Looks like nonsense—as
if some kid has been playing a typewriter."

Piper interrupted, told the lieutenant how to decode
the message by means of a typewriter keyboard. "One
space to the left."

There was another longish pause, and then the lieutenant said: "Here it is. Miss Withers says she's enclosing
pictures of the suspects in the case. Any one of these guys
might be somebody named D. L."

"Derek Laval. An old case in the 'Open' file. We had
him booked on suspicion of homicide and let him go. Go
on."

"And she wanted you to take the photos to whichever
one of the boys here at headquarters was assigned to the
case and see if he can identify Mr D.L."

Piper thought. "That would be Jack Nichols. Sergeant
Nichols then, but I think he's a captain now. Transferred to
Narcotics a couple of years ago. Check with him on the
pictures. He ought to remember the case—we had enough
headaches over it. And wire me here at the Tareyton
Hotel, Hollywood."

"Right," said the lieutenant.

"And, Georgie—what was the return address on that
envelope?" He waited eagerly for the answer.

"Return address—oh, here it is. 'Mammoth Studios,
Los Angeles.'"

"Nuts!" exploded the inspector, and hung up. "The
address is still a secret," he told Sansom. "But if everything goes well this case will be cracked in a couple of
hours. Hildegarde Withers had a brain wave. She drew
beards on photos of all the suspects and shipped 'em back
to Centre Street. If all goes well I ought to be on my way
East with my prisoner in a day or so."

Sansom brightened. "You mean—you want to take
this Laval back to stand trial for that old murder?"

"I want to take that trip back across country with Derek Laval in a train compartment," Piper said grimly. "I really look forward to that."

Sansom was definitely happier. "I'll co-operate with you one hundred per cent then. Because if we can avoid it we'd rather not have the whole thing dragged out here. Murder in a studio..." He shook his head. "Publicity shoots two ways sometimes."

"Then you'll help me with getting extradition?"

"Extradition, hell!" said Tom Sansom. "If we pick up the guy I'll toss him in my car and take the both of you over the state line into Arizona. Then you'll have first rights in the prisoner."

They shook hands on that, a bit prematurely, and the inspector sent out for sandwiches. Almost before they had finished a telegram arrived.

CAP NICHOLS PLAYING PINOCHLE DOWNSTAIRS. SAYS HE REMEMBERS HARRIS CASE PERFECTLY. ALWAYS THOUGHT LAVAL GUILTY. HESITATES TO MAKE POSITIVE IDENTIFICATION AFTER SO MANY YEARS BUT THINKS THREE IS BEST BET. SWARTHOUT.

"That's just dandy!" The inspector's sudden elation left him. Hildegarde's plan had worked like a charm— well, better than most charms. Only leave it to her to put numbers on the backs of the photographs instead of the names or initials of the suspects.

"You can have 'em sent back," Sansom suggested, "and check against the different people...."

Piper nodded. "Even air mail they wouldn't get here until late Tuesday, maybe Wednesday. That's no dice." It was one of the inspector's deepest beliefs that every hour of delay after the commission of a murder increases threefold the chances of the guilty person's escaping scot free. Time, he knew, is the criminal's best ally, time during which witnesses forget and clues grow cold and trails are covered up.

"Now we've got to find out where Hildegarde moved to," he told Chief Sansom. Because, he thought, she must have kept a record of the numbers on those photographs. No handbag had been found in the wreck of the studio courier car, but he doubted very much that she would carry anything really important around with her. Especially when she was so close to the killer.

"We can ask the boys down at the station to make a routine check of rooming houses, apartments and hotels," Sansom said. "But Los Angeles is a big place, sprawled all over southern California. And, besides, she might have moved to Santa Monica or Beverly Hills or Culver City."

Piper shook his head. "They wouldn't start a checkup today in this rain. I wouldn't do it myself. Besides, I'd like to get a little farther along before calling on the local police. You've got authority enough for us right now." Suddenly he snapped his fingers. "Yes—and you've got authority enough to put the bee on every taxi driver who has a stand near the hotel Miss Withers moved out of. She had bags, didn't she? Well, she wouldn't walk or take a streetcar. Come on."

Tom Sansom followed him, still dubious. "This ain't New York," he pointed out. "The taxicabs roam around a good deal. . . ."

That was putting it mildly. The doorman outside the Roosevelt said that half a hundred hackmen hung around outside at various times. They didn't keep regular stands but cruised here and there.

Then he gave them a ray of hope. It was when Piper asked him if he remembered putting a lady into a taxi on Wednesday evening. "She had London and Mexico City labels on her suitcases. Carried an umbrella probably— and she was probably wearing a hat that looked like a bird's nest."

The doorman brightened. "Wait! Maybe I remember——"

"Did she give you a dime tip?" Piper asked. The

other nodded. "That was Hildegarde!" cried Oscar Piper. "What cab did you put her into?"

The doorman shook his head. "How should I know? It was a Yellow—but practically every hack in Hollywood is a Yellow."

"So that's that," observed Tom Sansom. "Well, Inspector, I don't see what more we can do. If you ask me——"

"I'm asking the cab company," Piper said. "They usually make drivers keep a trip record. They're filed away somewhere at the company garage."

Sansom was still dubious. "Probably closed on Sunday. And I don't s'pose they'd be willing to look through all their records——"

"We won't ask 'em; we'll tell 'em," Piper said. "It usually works."

It worked. After considerable intensive research at the company garage the inspector discovered that Yellow taxicabs had picked up three fares at the Roosevelt during the hour when Miss Withers was known to have checked out of the place. One trip was to the new Union Station. One was to The Beachcomber's bar. And the last and most promising was to a number on Cowbell Canyon Drive.

They moved off, to the click of windshield wipers, into what seemed to be a minor waterfall. And finally Sansom pulled up beneath vast, untidy palm trees against a curb that was barely an inch above a roaring, muddy torrent.

"Could be *that* one," indicated Sansom. They slid out of the car and made a run for the archway. There a plump woman in a silk raincape was doing something to a list of tenants on the farther wall. Using a pair of manicure scissors, she pried out a card, threw it away.

"Looking for an apartment, gentlemen?" She turned toward them hopefully. "I'm Mrs Dermott, the manager here. I've got a nice double, just vacated. . . ."

Suddenly the inspector realized what apartment she must be talking about. He flashed his gold badge, hoping that she hadn't noticed the difference between the heraldry of Los Angeles and New York. "Police!" he said tersely. "That's the apartment we came to see you about. It was occupied by a Miss Hildegarde Withers, wasn't it?"

The woman stared at them blankly. "Whatever——?"

"It's all right. Will you show the way, please?"

"But that isn't the apartment I meant. I have another one vacant. Miss Withers paid me a month in advance and she didn't say anything about——"

"Okay, okay." The inspector followed the accepted police technique of never letting anyone have time to collect his thoughts. "Which way is it? The Withers' apartment, I mean?"

Mrs Dermott led the way, shaking her head. "Ten years in this business—you ask anybody around here—and this is the first time anyone of my tenants have ever been in any trouble with the police. . . ."

"All right, all right," the inspector told her. "You coming, Sansom?"

The other man seemed oddly reluctant. "Uh-huh, I guess so." He followed after, shaking the water from his topcoat.

"I hope there won't be any trouble. I mean, any publicity," Mrs Dermott rattled on. "Because I've had most of my tenants for years, and they're all the most respectable people, and——" She puffed up the stair. "What did she do? I mean, what is Miss Withers wanted for?"

"Just open the door for us," Piper ordered. "Thank you." He stood in the doorway, watching Mrs Dermott as the woman went uncertainly back down the stair. When she was out of sight and he was reasonably confident that she would not come sneaking back he opened the door, and the two men went inside.

The inspector liked to think that he was as unemotional and hard bitten as an old cavalry mule, that his years on the force of one of the wickeder cities of the world had made him immune to qualms. But he hesitated now, catching his breath.

For Hildegarde's rooms were faintly redolent of the lavender toilet water she always used. They were as neat and stiff and proper as that amazing lady herself. He had a feeling that he ought to wipe his feet dry on something, take off his hat and watch his grammar. It was definitely an uneasy feeling.

"So now we're here, what do we do?" Sansom demanded. "Pack up her duds?"

Oscar Piper frowned at him. The little living room in which they were standing showed Miss Withers' portable typewriter in its case on the desk, her handbag on the table. There was even a small blue bowl filled with dark red Jonathans on the table, and an ash tray held a neatly bitten white core.

Somebody else, decided the inspector, would have to pack up all these things and arrange for sending them back to Miss Withers' married sister. In Iowa or someplace, he thought. That melancholy task was something he would definitely avoid.

It was enough to search for her private notes and papers, to scout and peer and comb in the hope that she had left a record behind.

Especially of the numbers she had marked on those photographs. Well, they might as well get at it.

"You take the bedroom," Piper ordered. He himself picked up Miss Withers' handbag. Some silver, a few bills, the other half of her railway ticket, hairpins, a tiny flashlight and an employee's pass through the gates of Mammoth Studios. Trust Hildegarde not to keep anything of importance there.

He looked in the typewriter case. Nothing in the machine. Nothing but a wad of blank white typewriter paper in the compartment in the top of the case. The desk drawer held a bottle of ink and a blotter.

Piper felt definitely uneasy. Somehow things looked just a bit too neat, almost as if a stage had been set.

There was something wrong with the room. The knowledge came to him at once and of a sudden. He went to the window and looked out at the dreary slather of endless rain, at the sodden, dripping fronds of the anachronistic palm trees.

Nothing was wrong outside, barring the liquid sunshine. No balcony for anyone to be hiding on.

He came back, looked into the little closet by the door. Here was a hat, obviously one of Hildegarde's. Nobody else would wear a headpiece that resembled a full-rigged ship in a gale. There was also a coat, a sensible tweed coat which he recognized. Nothing in the pockets. Nothing under the shelf paper, nothing tacked to the bottom of the shelf.

But still something was wrong with the place. Some note was jarring, some detail was out of place in the primly neat picture. The inspector shook his head as if to clear it of cobwebs. Then he noticed the little wastepaper basket in the corner, went over to it and said: "Sansom!"

Tom Sansom appeared in the door of the bedroom. "Nothing in here that shouldn't be," he reported. "Just a bed and a chair and a bureau. Unless there's a false bottom in one of the suitcases."

"There isn't," Piper told him. He pointed. "Take a look at that."

Sansom peered into the wastebasket. "Don't tell me, let me guess. It's a cigar!"

Piper nodded. "Hildegarde didn't smoke. Especially she didn't smoke cigars. She wouldn't even let me into her apartment when I had a stogie going good."

They looked at each other. Sansom seemed amused.

"This is important," the inspector said. "Somebody has been here." He leaned over, picked up the cigar. "Still moist," he told the other officer. "Somebody has been here within the last half-hour!"

Tom Sansom looked very dubious. "We haven't found anything because somebody beat us to it!" insisted the inspector. "Somebody went through this place with a fine-toothed comb, and recently too." He pointed. "And there's more proof if you need it. That apple core there!"

Sansom scowled at it. "So it's an apple core. I don't see——"

"It's *white!*" The inspector smiled. "I happen to know that when the flesh of an apple is exposed to the air certain fruit acids make it turn brown within a few minutes. That apple was eaten within the last twenty minutes."

The other looked nervous. "Maybe the guy that did it is still here somewheres?"

Both men turned toward the door of the kitchenette. "Let's have a look," Piper demanded.

It was the first room in which they should have looked. They came through the doorway and stopped short, staring down at the linoleum floor. Starting at the back door and coming straight toward them across the linoleum was a line of footprints. They were large footprints, too large for a woman. And they were still wet.

"There!" said the inspector with a sort of weary triumph.

Sansom squatted down and stared at the prints as if he expected some revelation from their moist outlines. "Could be the houseboy," he suggested hopefully. "Some of these places have Filipino houseboys who come to cart away the trash. . . ." His voice trailed away doubtfully. Not even Tom Sansom could visualize a Filipino with feet that size—or one who would be doing his odd jobs on a Sunday afternoon.

There was no use searching the place any longer. They were stymied, and they knew it. "If we'd arrived a few minutes earlier we'd have nabbed somebody right here," Piper said as they came back into the living room.

Sansom shrugged. "Like the farmer's boy who said he *almost* heard the cowbell? Well, what's next, Inspector?"

"I don't know. If there was only some way of finding out what Hildegarde Withers was up to! She must have been on the verge of solving the whole mix-up, or the murderer wouldn't have struck at her. But if he's come back here and got hold of her notes..."

"The town's full of spiritualist mediums," Sansom said dryly. "They breed like flies in this part of the world. Or maybe you'd like to try to establish communications with your friend through the ouija board?"

Piper didn't answer that. "Some one of our suspects," he insisted, "is dodging back and forth between two identities. Jekyll and Hyde, or whatever it is. He's Derek Laval when he wants to be and then he's somebody else—some sober, respectable citizen that couldn't possibly do anything wrong."

The inspector scratched a match with his thumbnail and held the flame to his cigar. Outside it was twilight, a deep and murky twilight, but there was still light enough in the room to see Tom Sansom's face, thick and disbelieving.

"Well?" said the inspector.

Sansom shook his head. "I've about made up my mind that it's all goofer feathers. A guy falls off a chair and breaks his neck, and a driver goes off the road and kills himself and his passenger. Listen, Inspector, if we tried to work out a murder case whenever there's a fatal traffic accident in California..."

"I can't see that you're trying much in this case," Piper retorted.

"All right, all right. I'm not making trouble if I can help it. So far everybody's been talking murder and nobody's showed ten cents' worth of proof."

Piper looked at him quizzically. "Here then," he said. "This is just about ten cents' worth." And he took a small envelope out of his pocket, handed it to the studio officer.

Sansom looked inside. "Well? It looks like some sort of wax."

"It is. Sealing wax. I climbed down into Lost Lizard Canyon and ruined a suit of clothes to get that. Out of the death car."

"Now, listen, Inspector! You're not going to say that

the brakes on the courier car were sealed with sealing wax, are you?"

"Uh-uh. Not the brakes. But I found that somebody had taken the locking pin out of the steering post of that bus and substituted a hunk of sealing wax. That fitted right into the slot and it must have worked for quite a while. Then it cracked, degenerated into powder, and the wheel just spun around. Perhaps coming up into the higher altitude and the colder air would help. Anyway, one hard yank as they were turning a corner, and——" The inspector shut his eyes for a moment as if he had a sudden attack of headache.

Sansom still shook his head, but without real emphasis. He looked down at the contents of the envelope.

"The inspector is right," came a voice from behind them.

"Of course I'm——" Piper jerked his head around in a perfect double take. The hall door was ajar. Now it slowly, silently opened. In the doorway, clothed in something shimmery, silvery and unreal as moonbeams, stood Hildegarde Withers. She spoke.

"So *that's* how I was murdered!"

VIII

There will be time to prepare
A face to meet the faces that you meet,
THERE WILL BE TIME TO MURDER....

T. S. ELIOT

Plop! Plop! Plop! The drops of rain water fell from Miss Withers' cellophane raincape upon the hardwood floor. She came inside, shut the door behind her with a good, solid bang and switched on the light.

Tom Sansom, holding tight to the back of a chair, muttered something, but nobody was paying any attention to him. The inspector was just about the angriest man in the world at that moment, and his face was the shade of a plate of borsch.

"Oscar," said the schoolteacher gently, "you can't hold your breath forever, really you can't."

"I——" he began. "You——"

"I know, Oscar, I know," she went on quickly. "I'm not at all dead, and you're really very relieved about that. But also you're furious at me because you had that long trip out here and all the fuss and worry for nothing."

He still found it hard to say anything. "I'm sorry," Miss Withers went on. "I wired you not to worry no matter what you heard. I sent the wire to your home

115

because I thought that somebody might open and read it down at headquarters. . . ."

"I didn't even go home," he admitted. "I just hopped the first plane. . . ."

"Don't act like that. I *was* murdered, to all intents and purposes. Only I was lucky enough to pull down a folding bed on top of my head and knock myself cold. I was only unconscious for a few minutes, but it was long enough to make me miss connections with that studio car. Afterwards——"

"But listen, lady!" Tom Sansom objected. "Your body—I mean, the report and everything. How did you get the sheriff and the hospital to cover up for you? That doesn't make sense."

"They *didn't* cover up for me," she went on. "There was a woman in the studio car. A friend of the driver possibly. Or a hitchhiker that he picked up. . . ."

"Or the hotel chef's missing wife!" Piper interjected, remembering. "Of course!"

"Anyway, she was identified as being *I*. That was too good an opportunity for me to miss, because I had a strong feeling that the accident was not an accident and that someone was trying to get rid of me. So I kept out of sight and started sleuthing in earnest."

Piper said, "And you got——?"

She hesitated. "I don't quite know, Oscar. I can't tell yet." But she turned a little away from Tom Sansom, and her eyelid dropped.

"If you made any notes on your progress, somebody's been here and got them," Piper told her. "Because we've searched the place thoroughly, hoping against hope that you left something behind."

"Really, Oscar?" Miss Withers headed hastily for the kitchen. She threw open the refrigerator, took out a double boiler filled with cooked string beans and lifted the top. In the lower pan reposed a small notebook. "Perfectly safe, as I knew it would be. Besides, I haven't been gone long enough——"

"A man was in here," Piper insisted. "Those tracks on the kitchen floor"—he pointed—"and the apple."

"I'm afraid the tracks are mine," Miss Withers admitted, displaying her feet. She was wearing galoshes. "And I ate an apple just before I went out."

"Did you smoke a cigar just before you went out?" queried Tom Sansom.

The inspector told her about that. "No," said the schoolteacher, "I didn't smoke any cigar." She frowned. "I don't see how anybody could have left it there. I've had no men callers—and nobody even knows I'm living here."

"We found you," Piper said. "So someone else could."

He was looking for the cigar. But it wasn't in the wastebasket. It wasn't in any of the ash trays. "The thing's gone," he cried.

Then he saw the direction of Miss Withers' glance. She was staring at the cigar butt in his fingers.

"Good Lord! I must have lit it and smoked it without realizing——" Oscar Piper sat down suddenly in a chair, feeling foolish.

"Smoking is automatic for most people," Miss Withers reminded him. "It becomes such a habit that you have no idea of what your fingers are up to. Ten to one that is how the cigar got here in the first place. It smells just like those awful greenish-brown things you are so fond of."

Tom Sansom began to laugh. Once started, he found it hard to stop. Oscar Piper glared at the man and then could not help chiming in. He laughed until the tears filled his eyes.

"There's a time for everything." Miss Withers finally cut them short. "Have your hysterics, gentlemen, but remember that we are still faced with the problem of a murder. Right now, somewhere in this town, a man is congratulating himself on having perpetrated another successful crime. . . ."

"That's right," admitted Sansom soberly. "And I'd better get busy and report to Mr Lothian that you weren't killed in that wreck like we thought." He edged toward the door. "Maybe we can all get together for a conference sometime tomorrow?"

"Maybe we can," agreed the inspector.

When they were alone Miss Withers turned to him. "Oscar, it was sweet of you to drop everything and come rushing out here because you heard I was hurt. I do appreciate it—especially after the way we've always fought. . . ."

"What's wrong with a good fight?" he demanded. "It was this guy Laval I was after anyway. I hate having a case remain in the 'Open' file."

She smiled. "Of course, Oscar. By the way, I may have your case solved for you. I took a chance and dug up some photographs and set them to New York. . . ."

"I know," he told her. "That's what I was really hoping to find in your apartment—your notes on which picture was which suspect. Because I've already got a report on them from Centre Street."

She brightened. "Oscar! Did they manage to identify the man?"

"Captain Nichols remembers the case. He thinks it is number three in your retouched photos that looks most like the guy he arrested in the Harris case. Why, what's the matter?"

"Nothing's the matter," she said slowly. "Except that number three can't be the murderer of Saul Stafford—even if he does look well in an India-ink beard."

"Why not?"

"Because I decided that the experiment needed a control," she told him. "There weren't pictures enough. So I put in a photograph of Stafford himself—and *that was number three*."

The inspector gnawed absently at the dead end of his cigar. "Saul Stafford himself. Another blind alley." He told her about the abortive experiment at Lake Arrowhead. "That ended with Melicent Manning as the only suspect with the right type fingerprint."

Miss Withers was doubtful. "From what you tell me,

there was plenty of time for the colored man, Uncle Remus or whatever they called him, to switch glasses, substitute his own prints or anything else. Oscar, I'm afraid we haven't eliminated as many suspects as we had hoped."

"Now, Hildegarde——"

"They can be faked, as somebody or other proved last year with a gelatin process. Moreover, I myself saw the fingerprint evidence proving that both Sacco and Vanzetti handled the gun that killed the paymaster."

"That was Boston!" Piper snapped back.

"What can be faked in Boston can be faked in New York or Hollywood or anywhere else!"

Suddenly they both realized that they were yelling at each other. "Relax, Hildegarde, relax," Piper told her. "You're too het up for a ghost."

"Relax yourself, Oscar Piper," she came back. But she stopped, put her hand for a moment on his shoulder. "Say, how would you like to take me out to dinner tonight?—to celebrate my return from the Valley of the Shadow?"

He brightened. "Swell! Just like old times—nice, quiet place where we can talk this thing out over a dish of spaghetti and a bottle of red ink."

"Yes," Miss Withers said, smiling faintly, "spaghetti, by all means." She turned toward the bedroom door, then stopped. "Oscar, while I'm slipping into my best dress you might look at these letters I just got in answer to my ad in the newspaper. I asked for information about Derek Laval, hinting that it was to settle an estate."

The inspector took them. "Laval? I was beginning to think that his middle name was Yehudi. The little man who wasn't there."

Speedly Miss Withers brought him up to date on her research in the newspaper files. "Laval exists, as you see—and very active is the existence he leads. Any man who plays polo, stays up until dawn in the Swing Club, jitterbugs with young girls, et cetera and so forth——"

"It must be the climate," Piper told her, and settled

down to a study of the new exhibits. The first letter was unimportant, being only from a moving-picture extra player, named Jules Lavalliere, who thought that his name might originally have been Laval and who hoped for a modest share in the supposed Laval estate. The second was from the mother of a young lady, named Cecily, who had gone to San Francisco for the Labor Day week end with Derek Laval and had not been heard of since. Said mother would like a forwarding address so that she might send along Cecily's clothes, her parakeet and the small child which remained as a souvenir of Cecily's last elopement.

The third was even more puzzling, being from the editor of a local magazine, *Script*. He had, it seemed, several dozen manuscripts, mostly of verse, which had been submitted during the past year by Derek Laval, with no return address. Some of the titles were listed as *The Sterilized Heiress*, *The Self-Appointed Bastard*, *The Face on Mona's Floor* and *Owed to a Casting Couch*.

Mr Wagner, the editor, had found these poems not only unsuited to publication, but hesitated to undergo the risk of putting them back into the United States mail and would like the author to call for them in person.

"Obviously," Miss Withers announced as she swept out of the bedroom in her best dotted swiss, "Derek Laval is a person who ought to have his typewriter washed out with soap."

"Well, now——" objected the inspector.

But Miss Withers was frowning. "That's funny. He didn't have a typewriter when I searched his apartment downstairs. . . ."

The inspector did a double take on that. "You mean Laval *lives* in this building?"

"He did, but he doesn't any more. He called up the landlady yesterday and announced that he was going to give up the place. You coming, Oscar?"

Vaguely baffled, the inspector procured a taxicab and got her into it. And that was the end of their council of war, at least for the time being, because inevitably the driver smelled that they were visitors to southern California and set himself up as a guide. He even drove several blocks out of his way—or theirs—to point out Mae West's apartment house.

Finally, at an hour well past twilight, they whisked along that section of Sunset Boulevard which is known as "The Strip," from which vantage point all of western Los Angeles twinkled and sparkled below them like an illuminated map.

Even the inspector, not normally prone to enthuse about views, was forced to admit, "Maybe I've been wrong about the place." Then they slowed up for a traffic jam outside a great pink modernistic box of a building outlined with blue neon lights.

There was a gauntlet of sight-seers on either side of the velvet carpet leading to the door, cheering and waving autograph books. Flash bulbs popped steadily as the limousines and sport roadsters and motor scooters of the stars rolled up to the place.

"Big night at Shapiro's tonight," the driver told them. "It's the only place in Hollywood anybody important ever goes since the Trocadero folded. Tonight they're having a benefit dinner and special show—to buy ambulances to send to England. . . ."

"They need planes and tanks and destroyers, so we send ambulances," observed Miss Hildegarde Withers. Then, on an impulse—"Stop here, driver!"

He looked amazed. "But, lady, I was driving you out to Peppino's. This ain't no spaghetti joint. You don't want——"

"But I do."

Before the inspector could register a practical protest he found himself dragged willy-nilly through the gauntlet where Miss Withers had the surprising experience of being mistaken for Edna May Oliver and asked for an autograph.

"I think Shapiro's is going to be very interesting

tonight," the schoolteacher told Oscar Piper, and drew him firmly inside.

Jill Madison, an unripe orchid pinned in her hair because her silver gown had no shoulders, was dancing with Buster. They danced very close, moving as one person, not only because they were both young and felt the music all the way down to their toes but also because the dance floor at Shapiro's is always so crowded that all dancing is cheek to cheek. Almost any cheek.

"That's all, Buster," Jill said, and dropped her arms.

He held her resentfully. "You don't like the way I rhumba?"

"That wasn't a rhumba; it was a conga. And I haven't forgotten that I'm here with somebody else."

"With that Virgil Dobie!"

"That's right," she told him sweetly. "Now, don't be difficult. I'm trying to tell you to run along and peddle your papers."

"But, Jill——"

She stopped on the edge of the floor and for one moment she seemed to be relenting. But she wasn't—not Jill. "Now listen, sophomore," she said severely, "just because I run into you in the bar I dance with you. Can't you understand why? You're an awfully nice boy, and I'm sure that some awfully nice girl would just love to have you fall in love with her. . . ."

Buster's neat dinner coat suddenly seemed to shorten at the sleeves and hunch up at the back of the neck. "If you'd only——"

"I *won't* only! Please go away and stay away. I've got to get back to Virgil or——"

"So it's 'Virgil' now, is it?"

"Yes," Jill said. "I danced with you because I wanted to be nice. Our last dance together—like in Browning's poem."

"It was the last ride, not the last dance. 'We ride, and

I see her bossom heave, There's many a crown for who can reach . . . ' "

"Well!" exploded Jill, reddening under her make-up. She turned swiftly and marched toward the table where, under Virgil Dobie's approving stare, a waiter was spinning a bottle of Krug '28 in its silver bucket.

Buster shrugged and made his way back into the bar. People were lined up behind the brass rail like bettors outside the two-dollar win windows at Santa Anita, but he elbowed his way forward and eventually found himself standing beside a large, sultry girl in red and gold.

"Have a drink," he muttered, and then saw that it was Lillian from the studio. "Well, *do* have a drink."

"Oh, hello, Buster," she greeted him, a shade more warmly than usual. "I don't mind if I have a drink. I don't mind if I have six drinks. Stingers."

They began on the six stingers. Buster tried talking but he discovered that Lillian was not listening to him. He would have moved away, but she held him, putting her hand appealingly on his shoulder. "Stay with me for a while," she begged him. "I'll—I'll go Dutch on the drinks."

Somewhat puzzled, Buster wanted to know why. "You're not stagging it, too, are you?"

"No, I made old Josef bring me. He had two double martinis and folded up right in the middle of telling me a limerick about the young man from Khartoum. . . ."

Buster brightened, waiting.

"He's at the table in there," Lillian said. "If you want to hear the rest of it wake him up."

"Why not call a taxi and go home if he's that dull?"

Lillian drained her glass with a brisk intentness. "Oh no. I'm not going to walk out on my new boss. Wilfred Josef would never forgive that. Besides"—here she stopped and looked carefully around before continuing—"I came here to do something. Buster, tell me, how many drinks does it take to make you brave?"

"A good many, I should think. It might vary with the individual."

She nodded. "Then I'm going to stay right here and drink until I'm brave as anything."

The young man loosened his necktie. "I'm with you," he agreed. "At least until I fall off the stool."

He was nowhere near falling off the stool some time later when Thorwald L. Nincom arrived with a party of seven. There was Melicent Manning, Mona and Frankie Firsk, Harry Wagman the agent, a lovely hyperthyroid redhead whom Wagman hoped to sell for the part of Lizzie Borden, Willy Abend, wearing an American flag for a boutonniere, and Douglas August with his right hand in a vast white bandage.

"Nincom and his poops," Buster observed as the party swept past toward where a headwaiter guarded the door of the dining room. "I bet they have no reservation and I bet they get a table."

Buster was right. Mr Nincom and his party were awarded the signal privilege of having a table set up for them on the edge of the dance floor, but in spite of this they all seemed moderately unhappy.

Melicent Manning tried to make conversation, steering carefully away from topics which might upset Mr Nincom's digestion. "Do tell us about how you injured your hand, Douglas," she begged of Doug August. "I just know it was something romantic. You devil-may-care young men!"

"If you must know," August said, "it happened out on the polo field this morning——Oh, not in the game," he hastily added, realizing that Nincom was glaring at him. "I know I promised not to play while I'm on assignment. I was just practicing some stick and ball."

"Polo!" breathed Melicent Manning.

"But it *was* romantic," August continued. "You see, I dropped my mallet and got off my horse to pick it up, and the horse stepped on my hand."

There was a lull. "I knew a man once a horse *sat* on——" began Mona Firsk, and then her husband shushed her. Mr Nincom was about to speak. Or else choke to death with half a stalk of celery in his mouth. He was pointing over their heads, pointing toward the doorway, and emitting small gargling sounds.

"Look!" he finally got out.

Willy Abend peered. "Oh, it's Miss Withers, the lady who got killed. . . ." His voice trailed away into silence, and they all forgot to breathe for some seconds.

Back in the bar Buster Haight fell off his stool, but not from stingers.

It was no optical illusion. Miss Hildegarde Withers, in a neat dotted swiss, was arguing with the headwaiter. Beside her the inspector fidgeted, aware of how his trousers bagged.

"I am very sorry, madame, but without the reservation—"

"Speaking of reservations," Miss Withers plunged in, "can you tell me if Mr Derek Laval has a table for this evening?"

The dapper little man winced. "I am sorry, madame——"

"Flash it, Oscar," she suggested. The inspector flashed his badge, cupping it in the palm of his hand.

"Oh, I see," said the headwaiter. "No, I am glad to say, Mr Laval will not be among our guests. There is the matter of the checks, madame and monsieur, that he wrote last time. The bouncing checks."

That established, Miss Withers finally prevailed upon the man to give them a table, using all her persuasion and that of the inspector's badge and one of his five-dollar bills. This table, too, was set up on the edge of the rapidly diminishing dance floor.

Thus it was that the schoolteacher made her dramatic return from the wrong side of the river Styx into the middle of Shapiro's ballroom on a gala Sunday night, surrounded by the stars, starlets, executives and creators of Never-Never Land.

As they sat down she nodded and smiled at Mr Nincom and his guests who returned greetings as blank as those of a tableful of Humpty Dumpty toys.

And at a cozy table against the farther wall Jill Madison had to speak sharply to Virgil Dobie who kept on pouring priceless Krug '28 into her already brimming glass. On every side Miss Withers was making exactly the splash that she intended. It was a lovely idea, and one which she was to regret sincerely all the rest of her life.

But for a time all went serenely, with the vast roomful of diners hurrying through the fourteen courses of the table d'hôte—on which the inspector discovered spaghetti Caruso tucked in between the soup and the fish.

He also discovered, as have so many other tourists in Hollywood, that in real life Miss Irene Dunne looks smaller than on the screen, while Miss Myrna Loy looks larger, that Miss Greer Garson's beauty cries out for the color camera, that Mickey Rooney and Jackie Cooper are grown up now in some ways, especially as regards blondes, and that John Barrymore wears built-up heels and still looks considerably shorter than his current wife.

While the inspector was making these firsthand notes Miss Hildegarde Withers waited hopefully for the pay-off that she had been so sure of.

"I don't see why you think so," Piper objected when he learned her thoughts. "Suppose everybody else is here—the one man you want isn't around. Certainly the headwaiter would know—and he has reason for looking out for Derek Laval."

"Never mind Derek Laval," the schoolteacher said. "Watch."

The orchestra had left the stand, and now a committee of waiters were rearranging things so that a big square screen hung on the platform. When it was set in place they disappeared, and the band leader returned, held up his hand for attention.

"Ladies and gentlemen," he began, "you all know why we're here and you know that half of the cover charge and *take* tonight goes to a very worthy cause. And now for the special event on the program."

"If it's a torch singer I'm going," Piper whispered.

"By special arrangement with the newsreel companies and with the gracious permission of the Racing Commission for the sovereign state of California, we present a rerunning of the greatest horse race of all time, the Santa Anita Handicap!"

"That's Hollywood for you," Miss Withers whispered to the inspector as the lights slowly started to go dim. "Ninety per cent of the people in this room work in pictures all day. They have projection machines in their own homes, most of them. And for a special treat when they go to a night club they look at more motion pictures."

"Shhh!" grunted the inspector.

At the bar Lillian Gissing turned in dignified slow motion to her companion. "I think I'm pretty brave now," she announced heavily. "I think I'm as brave as I can get. If I have any more drinks . . ." She burped.

"You're sick," Buster said, mildly disinterested.

"I *am*. I'm pretty near as sick as I am brave. Maybe sicker. . . ."

"It's up there," Buster helpfully advised her, pointing. "At the head of the stairs and to the left along the balcony. Where it says 'Mesdames.'"

Lillian started away, careening slightly in the current. Then she rang for full speed astern and came back to pick up her handbag which she had left on the bar. She opened it, with a thickly suspicious glance at Buster, and made sure of something deep inside. Young Haight said later that he thought it was a piece of paper—maybe a card or an address, he couldn't tell.

Anyway, Lillian folded something into the palm of her hand, put the bag back on the bar to hold her place and went tacking off toward the stairs. The bar lights were very dim now, and Buster whirled on his stool to watch the screen in the larger room. . . .

The voice continued: "Not *just one* race, mind you, but each running of the Hundred-Thousand-Dollar Handicap, the richest race in the world, caught imperishably upon the silver screen as a record of thoroughbred stamina and—and——Well, anyway, we've got the films up in the projection booth, and they'll be run off in sequence. Take it away. . . ."

The room was dark now except for the pale red exit lamps, and time suddenly turned backward to a day in March 1935 when sixty thousand people filled the new grandstand at Arcadia and watched a field of thoroughbreds thunder down across what was once the peaceful pasture of Lucky Baldwin's breeding ranch. Head Play and Twenty Grand and Mate. . . .

Again on the screen the greatest horses in America fought for racing's richest prize, and again a rank outsider, a reformed jumper of no repute, came tearing out in front to stay in front. That was Azucar's year.

Virgil Dobie looked at Jill. "That was the day I had a hundred and eight dollars in the world, and the hundred was on Twenty Grand to win." He shuddered. "I think I'll feel my way out to the bar and see a man about a brandy and soda."

On the big screen in the ballroom it was 1936 now, with a landscaped infield at Santa Anita, more grandstand, more people and more sunshine. Discovery and Time Supply and old Azucar again. . . .

And the recorded voice of Joe Hernandez booming out his unforgettable "Ther-r-r-r-re they go!" with the crowd roaring, the thunder of hoofs as the field came into the homestretch. . . .

Again on the screen the front-running son of Peanuts was pulled to the rail to foul three challengers and win a hollow victory, with Time Supply, a faster horse, running up his heels. That was the year that Top Row stole the "hundred grand."

At Mr Nincom's table the great man spoke into the darkness. "I have an idea," he cried. "It's about time for another race-track epic. We'll call it—we'll call it 'Kentucky.' No, not 'Kentucky.' Why plug those Eastern states? We'll call it 'Santa Anita'!"

"Marvelous!" came Frankie Firsk's voice. "A *real* honey. . . ."

"Swell," chimed in Doug August. "Only I thought you said that race-track pictures always lose money because the women don't like 'em?"

Nincom coughed. "Did I? Well——" He brightened. "We'll build the story around a woman handicapper—get the woman's angle that way. She has a running battle with a gyp owner and trainer, a hard-boiled Gable type. She loves horses; he thinks of them as meal tickets only. But when he tries to pull a sneak and win the Handicap with a horse he flies in from south of the border . . ."

The people at the side tables and in the benches along the wall were crowding forward now, taking up positions on the dance floor and steps for a better view. A few moved back and forth from the murky bar. Another year, another field of horses—and gallant Rosemont slipping past in the last eighth of a mile to grab the race from little Seabiscuit.

Still another year, with the grandstand stretching farther up the track and the infield festooned with geometrical flower beds. And a Latin-American thunderbolt, named Kayak II, chalking up his win. Then a Sande-trained three-year-old, weighted with a feather, flew down the homestretch as Seabiscuit, the unlucky, coasted in for a win and nipped him at the wire. Stagehand wore the flowers that day. . . . The entertainment committee realized by now that the program was being a tremendous failure as well as a howling success that night at Shapiro's. It was a failure in that nobody was remembering to keep on ordering drinks or food, a success in that for that brief hour every guest and every employee in the place lost himself completely.

There on the screen were flashing the most breath-taking moments of the turf's last six years, the summit of man's gambling urge and horses' courage and endeavor. It was a program all of climaxes, one which wrung its audience out and left them limp as dishrags.

Afterwards nobody knew what time it was. Nobody knew exactly where he had been sitting or whose glass he had drained. By the time homely little Seabiscuit, twice cheated of his triumph, romped home on his gimpy old legs to win the Handicap for 1940 and become the greatest money winner of all time there was not—as the saying goes in Hollywood—a dry seat in the house.

When the lights came on everyone was applauding. Miss Withers and the inspector, Thorwald Nincom and his whole tableful—even Virgil Dobie and Jill were clapping, his right against her left, because at the same time they were holding hands under the table. The crowd kept on applauding as if they were going to insist on Seabiscuit's taking a bow on the stage.

Then the roar of clapping hands died away, an audible silence spreading from the doors out and across the ballroom. Heads turned, people frowned, jerked back to reality. . . .

There was something wrong out in the bar, some false note. The whisper ran from table to table, and people began to rise uncertainly. Photographers deserted their celebrities and ran across the dance floor, screwing fresh flash bulbs into their cameras. . . .

It seemed that when the lights came back on somebody had noticed a girl lying on a big divan at the far side of the bar—a lush, dark girl partially undressed in red and gold. At first they thought that she was simply blotto and then they saw the red-gold rag caught on the balcony rail thirty feet above.

Nobody had seen her come out of the powder room. Nobody had heard anything, which wasn't odd, considering the volume to which Mr Hernandez' voice had been amplified. Nobody had noticed anything out of the way at all. And yet there she was.

All that anybody could be sure of was that Lillian's neck was broken.

IX

And **I HAD DONE A HELLISH THING,**
And it would work 'em woe....

SAMUEL TAYLOR COLERIDGE

"Los Angeles Police...calling car 17...car 17.... Call your station. That is all."

The radio sergeant called Hollywood substation, speaking a bit thickly because he had one of Shapiro's "Special Blend" cigars in his mouth.

"Yeah, we come out here. Nothing to it. A dame just got lit up and fell offen a balcony. Name, Lillian Gissing; age, 24; address, Studio Club. Dead on arrival. What?"

The sergeant chewed deeply into his cigar, a frown creasing his smooth brown forehead. "Huh? Oh. Well, we talked to the maid who hangs out in the powder room. That's what they call the can. Yeah. Big jigaboo right outa *Gone with the Wind*. She says she remembers this dame coming into the place spiffed. Tried to get her to take a fizz but all she could get down her was aspirin. A little while later while they were running some films downstairs she notices that the Gissing dame is sitting on a bench out on the balcony, about passed out. So she goes down to the kitchen to get her a cupa cawfee and when she comes back she's gone. Yeah. Musta got dizzy and fell over. Left

131

a hunka her dress caught on the balcony grillwork. Okay?"

He was about to hang up, but a question from the station stopped him cold. "Huh? No, of course nobody seen her. The lights in the place was turned down way low, and everybody was looking at the films. Nobody heard nothing neither. But they had the amplifier for the picture sound track turned way up high, and, besides, the Gissing dame lit on a big overstuffed couch. Yeah, only her head musta hit the back or something. Yeah. The way I figure it is——"

No matter how the sergeant figured it, matters were almost immediately taken out of his horny hands. For now the short, angry snarl of a squad-car siren sounded outside the glittering portals of Shapiro's, and two serious-looking men entered without handing their hats to the checkroom girl. Or, for that matter, without taking their hats off. They were followed by a uniformed detail.

The sergeant recognized them at once as a lieutenant and a sergeant from Homicide Bureau downtown and realized that the case which he had just washed up so neatly and so much to the satisfaction of the management was reopened again. But good.

"Somebody phoned in a beef," was all the information he received as the lieutenant sent him back to cruising.

It must have been a very convincing beef because a few minutes later Coroner Panzer arrived, wearing the top of his pajamas for a shirt. He, too, looked extremely serious.

The management was annoyed. The guests were annoyed, those of them who had remained after the unfortunate accident which now appeared to be something else again. Most annoyed of all the guests was Thorwald L. Nincom when he was advised that the presence of himself and his party was requested upstairs in the banquet room. Mr Nincom threatened to telephone to Mayor Bowron; he threatened to telephone to Governor Olson. "Do you know who I am?"

The officer knew and he was very unhappy about it. But it would take only a few minutes.

When Mr Nincom and his guests reached the small banquet room upstairs they found that a number of other interested, and interesting, parties were there. Among them were Virgil Dobie and Jill, young Buster Haight and Mr Wilfred Josef.

"I'm not going to say anything without a lawyer present," Willy Abend was insisting. "According to the Bill of Rights——"

"Willy, be quiet!" cried Melicent Manning. "Don't you see what's happening? We're being murdered off, one by one. . . ."

Mona Firsk leaned close to her husband. "Frankie, you don't think that one of *us* is—you know, the murderer?"

He shrugged.

"I don't suppose it's you," she whispered, a faint note of disappointment in her voice. "You wouldn't have the nerve."

Douglas August said nothing, but sat and picked quietly at the edge of his bandage.

Harry Wagman, the agent, made one or two futile attempts to draw Mr Nincom into a conversation about the abilities and charms of the hyperthyroid redhead who sat beside him with her hands folded and stared wonderingly at everything. After a while an officer came and told her that she could go. Which she did, briskly. It was quite obviously no time to work on Mr Nincom, no matter how suitable she might be for the part of Lizzie Borden.

And the door of the manager's office remained firmly closed, though now and then the faint rumble of voices sounded within. Finally a fat and self-righteous colored woman emerged, then hurried out as if the bloodhounds were after her.

Virgil Dobie and Jill stared at each other, and Buster Haight stared at Jill. The silence grew thicker and thicker.

From the ballroom downstairs they could hear the orchestra for a while, and then that, too, died away. Festivities at Shapiro's were definitely over for the evening. A waiter came up past the bored officer who guarded the door and wanted to know if anybody wanted to order a drink or anything before they closed the bar.

"If it's all right . . . ?" Frankie Firsk said dubiously, looking at the law.

"Go ahead—my only instructions is to keep you here." So they all had drinks, with the exception of Virgil Dobie.

"I think I'll stick to ginger ale," he said to Jill, and did.

There was a little flush of conversation while the drinks were being tossed off, and then the silence was heavy upon them again. Josef, he of the singed beard, broke it momentarily when Buster Haight struck a match to a cigarette close beside him. "Don't do that!" shrieked Mr Josef. "I can't stand being near fire again." And he gave a sidelong glance at Virgil Dobie.

"Sorry," Dobie said. "Well, I—I'm sorry." There didn't seem to be much of anything more to say. Buster took his cigarettes and matches to the other side of the room and resumed his close study of the way Jill's eyelashes swept upward from her cheek.

Then suddenly the office door opened, and out came the two homicide detectives, the lieutenant still wearing his hat. With them, and evidently on good terms, was Inspector Oscar Piper. And Miss Withers.

A great light dawned on Mr Nincom. "I might have known it!" he cried accusingly. "*You're* responsible for our being kept here while everybody else went home. You and your fantastic ideas——"

"All right, all right," said the man with the hat. "We won't keep anybody long. . . ."

Mr Nincom turned to Harry Wagman, his face mottled with red. "She's fired!" he gave out in a stage whisper.

"She's got a contract," Wagman retorted. "Iron bound."

"Staying away two days voids the contract!"

"All right, please!" said the lieutenant again. "That can wait. All we want to know is, what do you know about this Lillian Gissing?"

Nobody said anything.

"Who saw her last?"

Again nobody said anything. Buster Haight put his cigarette out and deposited the butt neatly in the cuff of his trousers. Then he realized that somebody was pointing at him. It was Virgil Dobie.

"I saw her with that kid at the bar," he said.

Buster answered questions for ten busy minutes. All he knew was that Lillian had been drinking pretty heavily because she wanted to get brave. And she'd taken something out of her purse and gone upstairs. . . .

He hadn't seen her again. But he'd been watching the pictures. Like everybody else.

"Do you think she had an appointment with somebody?" the inspector put in.

Buster didn't think so. "She just wanted to get brave. . . ."

The two local detectives looked at each other and nodded. Oscar Piper nodded, too, though not quite as firmly. "Seems pretty clear that she was trying to get brave enough to commit suicide, then," said the sergeant.

"Yeah, and that would account for her not screaming when she fell. People don't yell when they know they're going to fall."

"Are we to be kept here all night while we listen to the reasons why a stenographer took her own life in a fit of drunken melancholia?" burst in Mr Nincom.

The officers looked at each other and then at the inspector. "Well," said the lieutenant slowly, "much as we'd like to play ball with you fellows in the big town . . ."

Piper looked around for Miss Withers, but she wasn't in view. A moment later they heard from her in the shape of a commotion outside on the balcony, the sound of running feet, the irate voice of a policeman and then a tremendous crash.

Miss Withers' voice came triumphantly above everything else. "Look!" she was crying. "Look at that!"

When Piper got out onto the balcony he looked down into the empty bar, straight down where an ornamental pot holding a small orange tree now reposed in the center of a collapsed divan.

"She threw it over——" began the guardian of the door in a very injured tone. "Just ups with it, and over it goes!" He held Miss Withers' arm with a firm grip.

"Of course I did!" insisted that lady, still triumphant. "That pot couldn't have weighed over a hundred pounds, or I wouldn't have been able to lift it. But look—it was heavy enough to break the legs of that divan downstairs. And you mean to stand there and tell me that a hundred-and-thirty-pound girl could land on it without any damage at all?"

"Leave go of her," said the lieutenant wearily as he took off his hat and mopped his head. "I'm afraid she's right."

"She didn't fall," agreed his partner slowly. "She didn't jump and she wasn't pushed."

"And somebody tore off a piece of her dress and hooked it on this balcony so it would look as if she fell!" the schoolteacher continued. "Which makes it add up to murder."

Behind them, from the door marked "Mesdames" appeared Dr Panzer, with his sleeves rolled up. "She's right," said the coroner. "About the girl not falling anyway. She hasn't got a bruise on her body, so she didn't fall thirty feet. But her neck's broken."

"Or, in other words," interrupted Miss Hildegarde Withers dryly, "she has a fracture dislocation of the second cervical vertebra and lesion of the spinal cord?"

Coroner Panzer stared at her. "Why—yes," he admitted. "I mean——But——"

"I'm only quoting your own report from your examination of the body of Saul Stafford," the schoolteacher explained. "I can remember the rest of it too. Let me see—'Anterior surface of the body—negative. Abdominal cavity . . .'"

"Wait a minute," cut in Dr Panzer. "Lady, I don't know who you are or how you got in this thing——"

"Neither do I," grinned the lieutenant. "But go on, Doc."

"Anyway," said Dr Panzer, "there's one difference between the Stafford case and this Gissing girl. I'll show you."

He beckoned, led the way back through the door into the powder room where the body of Lillian Gissing was laid neatly out on a lounge. Briskly and impersonally Dr Panzer drew back the sheet to disclose the dead girl's face. "Notice the marks on the cheek," he said, pointing with his pencil. "One, two, three, four—four fingernail scratches on her left cheek, running from jawbone to ear."

"Meaning violence?" demanded the lieutenant.

Panzer shrugged. "It could be. Or the girl could have clutched her own face"—he demonstrated—"like this."

"She couldn't break her own neck, could she?" demanded Inspector Oscar Piper.

The lieutenant hastily introduced them. "Inspector Piper is out here from New York on account of an old case of his—where a woman got her neck broken from a five-foot fall."

Panzer frowned deeply. "Three cases, eh? Well, maybe. But I don't believe that it is physically possible for any person to break another's neck. The neck muscles are too strong——"

The inspector nodded. "That's what our own medical examiner has always maintained."

"It could be done with an iron bar or some such device," the coroner went on thoughtfully. "But no matter how you'd pad it, that would leave contusions, rupture blood vessels underneath the skin. No, outside of a hard fall, I don't see how such injuries as these could be caused."

"Well," pointed out Miss Withers, "the scratches on her left cheek were not caused by Lillian Gissing herself. Because there are four of them—and look at her hands."

They looked and saw that Lillian's fingernails were long and heavily coated with geranium polish—all but one nail on the left hand and two on the right which had been broken off short and repaired by pasting the broken nail back again. "Any strain on that repair job would have torn the pasted nail off," she said, and demonstrated.

"Maybe this job was done by a woman!" spoke up the sergeant hopefully.

Oscar Piper shook his head. "Men have fingernails too. And whoever Derek Laval may be, we know he's a man." He explained to the local officers. "We had him in the clink once on suspicion and had to let him go for lack of evidence."

The lieutenant said that he would put out a general alarm on Derek Laval right away. "That ought to bring him in within twenty-four hours unless he's skipped town."

Miss Withers wasn't so sure. A strange conviction about Mr Laval was beginning to grow in her mind. A new and surprising and somewhat preposterous conviction that she could not get rid of.

A uniformed man appeared, saluted and told the lieutenant that the people in the banquet room were about at the boiling point and that the manager of the place wanted to know how long he would have to keep open for them.

"I guess we'd better turn 'em loose," said the lieutenant. "Eh, Inspector? We haven't got enough on anybody to hold them and we can always pick up any of this crowd of celebrities."

"I think you're right," Piper agreed.

But Miss Withers was in the throes of an inspiration. "Just one more minute!" she breathed. "Did I hear somebody say that the manager was still around?" She dusted her hands together. "Then it's easy! Why didn't I think of it before! All we have to do is to make each of those people in the other room—suspects, I suppose you'd call them—write down his own name and address. . . ."

It took her ten minutes to win her point. Getting the signatures was easy enough, except for Douglas August who displayed his bandaged hand. "I've never cultivated the knack of writing with the left," he explained.

"Mr August was injured practicing polo this morning," Melicent Manning explained somewhat unnecessarily.

For a moment everything spun around Miss Withers like a maelstrom. She remembered a photograph of two men riding hell-bent down the Riviera field. . . . And one was Derek Laval.

"Relax, Hildegarde," the inspector whispered to her. "Suppose the guy can't give you the sample signature you're looking for? With only one hand he certainly didn't commit any murders today!"

"Hmmm," said the schoolteacher, her eyes narrowing. "Watch, Oscar."

And she bore down upon Douglas August, pretended clumsily to trip and clutched at his bandaged hand. Whatever result she had expected was not the one she got, for that gentleman closed both eyes and let out an anguished bellow of pain.

It was no job of acting. August really did have an injured hand—that much was sure. She made hasty apologies and withdrew.

The ruffled little herd of suspects filed down the stairs past the wrecked divan and out through the darkened and deserted bar.

Buster Haight watched Jill hopefully, but she showed no signs of requiring a ride home. In fact, she climbed into Virgil Dobie's red cut-down Packard with a happy, childlike eagerness and snuggled against his arm as they roared away.

"Now that that's over," Dobie said to the girl as they

slipped along Sunset, "suppose I feed you? I can't sleep now and I don't suppose you can either."

"No," said Jill in the smallest of voices.

"Where would you like to eat? The Derby? A drive-in somewhere?"

She shook her head. "Somewhere far," said Jill.

Virgil Dobie thought a minute. "I know a swell place," he said. "And it's far." He slid his arm along the back of the seat, and her head settled firmly against his big shoulder.

Far behind them, in the little office on the second floor of Shapiro's, three officers and a maiden schoolteacher were poring over a problem in handwriting identification. Before them reposed samples of every signature but one among tonight's suspects plus two checks, signed "Derek Laval" and stamped "NSF" in large red letters inside a black square, which the manager had produced from his safe.

It was evident from the beginning that none of the samples matched the checks. Even the sergeant knew enough about the fundamental handwriting characteristics to see that the variance was wide as a barn door.

"It's that guy August, all right," decided the lieutenant. "We'd better pick him up—"

"Wait a minute," muttered Miss Hildegarde Withers. "Please wait a minute!" She was staring at the two worthless checks. Suddenly she put them down, turned to the officers. "As if it weren't bad enough that none of our handwriting samples matches the checks—has it occurred to any of you that the checks *don't even match each other?*"

She was right; they were forced to admit that. Among his many other accomplishments it appeared that Derek Laval had the ability to sign his name in two entirely different and distinct handwritings!

That, at least for the time being, brought the investigation up against a stone wall.

It was a stone wall against which, all the rest of that

night, Miss Withers butted her head. She was haunted by that well-known will-o'-the-wisp about town, Mr Derek Laval. He materialized and dematerialized. He made telephone calls and wrote checks and played polo and got raided in night clubs. He went jitterbugging with young ladies, and his past included a session in New York's Greenwich Village during which he wrote poetry and lost his sweetheart through a broken neck.

And yet he never existed. Not really. When she got anywhere near him he dissolved into shadows. When she was about to touch him he went screaming off with the wind, like the terrible windigo of the North Woods, the phantom thing that runs above the tops of the pines.

X

We shall know what the darkness discovers
IF THE GRAVE-PIT BE SHALLOW *or deep....*

Algernon Charles Swinburne

After a night spent in exercising a particularly virulent variety of nightmares Miss Hildegarde Withers finally drifted off into a sodden, peaceful sleep, deep in which Professor Jastrow calls the "universal unconsciousness."

And, as was usual with that lady when she went to sleep with a problem occupying her mind, she woke up with an answer. Perhaps not *the* answer. But, then, it was not given to her to look in the back of the book as if this were an algebra problem or a mystery story and find out for sure.

Yet an answer, even the wrong answer, was something at this stage of the game. It was the beginning of the end—she could sense it; she could feel it in what she was wont to describe as her bones.

The schoolteacher seized the telephone and got through to the inspector at the Hotel Tareyton.

"But, Hildegarde!" he protested. "I haven't even had a cup of coffee yet, and you want me to start sending wires to New York. Besides, the boys back at headquarters will think I'm out of my mind. . . ."

"It's hardly a sleeper jump," she said acidly. "Oscar, will you please do as I say? Because I have a hunch."

Before the inspector had even been allowed a decent length of time in which to be wheedled she had hung up. Miss Withers had other calls to be made this morning, and the most important one was to Dr John Panzer, chief coroner of the county of Los Angeles.

"You want me to *what?*" demanded that worthy gentleman when she had finally run him down.

"Not to *what*. I want you to have the body of Saul Stafford exhumed. That isn't such a complicated matter, is it? People get exhumed every day."

"But, my dear lady, there is a lot of red tape——"

"Red tape, fiddlesticks. Why, I was reading only the other day about a case in Philadelphia. They dug up a body in the middle of the night, and the murderer horned in and performed the autopsy on his own victim. It was a man named H. H. Holmes. . . ."

"I know, I know," said Dr Panzer wearily. "His real name was Herman Mudgett. But that was years ago. Nowadays it takes an order from the district attorney—which Mr Buron Fitts isn't likely to hand out to somebody he doesn't know—or an order from an immediate member of the family. And Saul Stafford had no immediate family. So——"

"But that body has to be exhumed," cried Miss Withers. "I insist! I——"

Then she stopped talking long enough to learn that exhumation would not be necessary for the reason that the mortal remains of Saul Stafford had not yet been consigned to their last resting place. Instructions from distant relatives in British Columbia were still being awaited.

"Then you *can* take his fingerprints!" Miss Withers cried happily.

Dr Panzer explained very wearily that the fingerprints of a person who died mysteriously were always taken in the morgue as a matter of course. Saul Stafford's prints were on record. For that matter, the doctor thought that he had them right here on his desk. Which he did.

"Well," said Miss Hildegarde Withers. "Doctor Panzer, do you know enough about fingerprints to know what a lateral pocket loop might be?"

Dr Panzer thought that he did.

"I don't suppose," she continued, "that Saul Stafford had a lateral pocket loop on any finger of his right hand?"

"Why"—and there was a longish pause—"as a matter of fact, he has. Or had, if you prefer. Why?"

"Thank you so much," said Miss Withers swiftly, unconsciously quoting Mr Charlie Chan. And she hung up.

What with one thing and another, it was nearly noon before she heard from the inspector. But his news was worth waiting for.

"Hildegarde, what do you think!" he chortled. "It's been checked and double checked. And, strange as it seems, believe it or not, the boys report from Centre Street that every officer who had anything to do with the arrest of Derek Laval in the Harris case eight years ago and every turnkey and guard and warden who had anything to do with the jug where he was kept swears that photograph number three is the guy they held!"

Miss Withers caught her breath sharply but she didn't say anything.

"Hildegarde, do you realize what that means?" he cried. "We've got positive evidence that Saul Stafford and Derek Laval were one and the same guy. In other words . . ."

"In other words, Saul Stafford was the man who murdered him. He was his own victim and his own murderer. Is that it?"

"Well," Piper admitted, "it looks that way now——"

"This wasn't suicide," said the schoolteacher gently.

"And they weren't one and the same person. No man in this world could break his own neck, Oscar."

Now it was the inspector's turn to be silent.

"I'm still trying to figure out how a man could break *another's* neck without leaving a mark," she went on. "If we could figure out that we'd be at least somewhat *forrader*."

She hung up on the inspector and called the studio again. When she finally got through to Gertrude at the third-floor Writers' switchboard she asked once more for Virgil Dobie.

"He hasn't come in yet," was the answer.

"Very well," said Miss Withers. "When he does would you ask him to call Miss Hildegarde Withers at——?"

"Oh, Miss Withers," Gertrude cried. "We've been trying to get in touch with you all morning. You're wanted in the front office. . . ."

"I know—they want to advise me that I'm fired," said the schoolteacher. "Never mind that. I only want to get in touch with Mr Dobie. Have him call me at Bowling Green 5-1123."

The phone buzzed back almost immediately, but it was not Virgil Dobie as she had hoped. Miss Withers heard the voice of her erstwhile agent, Harry Wagman.

"Listen," he greeted her, "get down to the studio as quick as you can. Mr Lothian wants to see you."

"But I was fired last night. You heard Mr Nincom say——"

"He was mad," Wagman said. "You haven't had as much contact with genius as I have. He didn't mean it, and, besides, Mr Lothian can buy and sell Nincoms by the dozen. So get down there."

She got. Mr Lothian saw her at once in his private office, looking more than ever like a small-town banker. Only now he was a banker with stomach ulcers.

Finally he worked his way around to the point. "This is very hard to put into words——" he began.

"Not at all," said Miss Hildegarde Withers. "You

want to tell me that I'm fired from my job as technical adviser and you want to point out that the police are in charge and that it would be a good idea for me to stop sleuthing——"

"No," said Mr Lothian. He fiddled with the pens on his desk. "On the contrary. The police *are* investigating. But they think the whole thing is a cock-and-bull story. What is a cock-and-bull story, by the way?"

Miss Withers said that she would look it up in *Aesop's Fables* for him. "Anyway," continued Mr Lothian, "they point out that everything that happened is capable of a natural explanation. Saul Stafford could have broken his neck falling off the chair. Our studio driver and his passenger who was mistaken for you could have gone off the road into Lost Lizard Canyon by accident. Lillian Gissing could have fallen off that balcony by accident. . . ."

"Except that she didn't, and I can prove it!" Miss Withers told him.

"Exactly. This series of *accidents* has got to stop."

"I'm afraid that it won't," she confessed. "The records show that a really clever murderer keeps on until he's caught. It's sort of egomania with a terrific compulsion to repeat and repeat. . . ."

Again Mr Lothian nodded. "That is what we're afraid of." He carefully lighted a cigarette and ground it out immediately in his big black marble ash tray. "The point is, how can you break people's necks without leaving a mark?"

She nodded. "My father used to tell a story about Paul Bunyan and the way he killed an eagle. The eagle sat on the stump of a dead tree and never took his eyes off Paul Bunyan. So Paul ran around the tree so fast that the eagle wrung its own neck. But I don't think that happened in the case of Saul Stafford, or the girl either."

Mr Lothian stared at her. "But you must have some theory about this case. . . ."

"A complete set," she admitted. "Though I haven't had time to check up on much of anything."

"How would you like to have time enough? How would you like to have the studio retain you to work this thing out? You would ostensibly continue your work for Mr Nincom as technical adviser, with a free hand and an unlimited—within reason—expense account."

She said somewhat blankly that she would like that very much.

"It's settled, then," said Mr Lothian. He took a small white card from his pocket, scribbled something on it. "This will be your authority," he told her. "Use it only when you must. . . ."

"'Whatever the bearer hereof has done he has done for the good of the state,'" quoted Miss Withers. "That's what it used to say on a *carte blanche*, at least according to Dumas."

"Uh-huh," agreed Mr Lothian somewhat absently. "Now, just what will be your first course, Miss Withers?"

"I'm not sure," she admitted. "But I think it might be a good idea to have a nice long heart-to-heart talk with Virgil Dobie."

Which was more difficult than she had imagined. Because when she had finally been readmitted to the little circle of Nincom writers she found Virgil Dobie among the missing.

"He hasn't even telephoned in or made any explanation whatever," complained Thorwald L. Nincom. "This disappearance act seems to be an epidemic among our little group——"

Miss Withers sensed that he was staring at her and smiled meekly. And the story conference continued. Mr Nincom was at the moment involved with the problem of the murder weapon to be used in his re-creation of the Borden case.

"Perhaps Miss Withers can advise us," he suggested. "Just what sort of an ax was it, according to the records?"

"I beg your pardon?" Hildegarde Withers wasn't thinking about axes. She was, as a matter of fact, looking at fingernails. At Frankie Firsk's claws, bitten down to the quick. At Willy Abend's, only a shade better, and at Doug August's squared-off nails projecting from his bandage. . . .

Mr Nincom, somewhat testily, repeated the question. "Oh," said she. "It wasn't really an ax at all, in spite of the poem. It was a small hatchet."

Every face in the room fell.

"A *hatchet?*" echoed Mr Nincom. Miss Withers nodded.

"Maybe it was an Indian tomahawk—we could take that liberty, and nobody would know!" cried Frankie Firsk.

"No," said Nincom. "Not a hatchet and not a tomahawk. This picture is going to be a Thornwald L. Nincom special, and everything in it has to be *big*. We'll have Lizzie use an ax—a big shining, double-bitted ax!"

Melicent Manning shook her head sadly. "I still think we ought to leave it up in the air whether Lizzie committed those murders or not. It doesn't seem right to me that a woman would kill anybody like that. . . ." She patted her hair with fingers tipped by chipped rose-tinted nails—long nails that added inches to her flabby fingers.

Miss Withers shook her head sharply to bring her mind back to the matter at hand. "Or a halberd," Mr Nincom was saying, a light in his eye. "One of those antique things, like an ax, only twelve feet long, with a blade like a plow!" He turned on the technical adviser. "Wouldn't it be plausible that the Borden family, with all their shipping business, would have collected a lot of antique armor and weapons, so that the murderer could pick a halberd off the wall? It would be more picturesque."

The schoolteacher winced. How could she picture for them the Borden house with its tiny square rooms, its haircloth sofas and wax flowers under glass? "I'm afraid not," she told him. But Mr Nincom wasn't listening.

"A halberd!" he repeated. "Now we've got something with production value! I want Dobie to write the scene this afternoon, lay it on thick. Lizzie, like an avenging angel, with the halberd held high over her head. . . ." He stopped. "That is, if the fellow condescends to come to work." Nincom pressed a button. "Smythe, call Virgil

Dobie's office and ask that secretary of his if she's heard anything from him. Is he coming in today or isn't he?"

There was a short lapse of time during which Nincom elaborated on his plans for the halberd. And then the phone rang. "Yes?" he barked, clenching the receiver with fingers that were tipped by longish yellow claws.

A rosy flush crept over the face of Thorwald L. Nincom. "Oh, really!" he rasped. "So Miss Madison hasn't seen fit to show up for work either? What goes on here anyway?"

"You're not the only one who is wondering," said Miss Withers softly, and tiptoed swiftly out of the sanctum sanctorum.

Up on the third floor of Writers' there was little enough information. Neither Virgil Dobie nor his secretary had appeared for work—that was all. Nor reported sick.

Miss Withers cut short Gertrude's efforts to discuss the tragedy of last night. "Do me a favor," she begged. "Try to get Mr Dobie at his home."

The plump girl plugged in on her board, dialed a number. "No answer at Mr Dobie's apartment," she reported. "Miss Withers, do you really think that Lillian——?"

"I haven't had time to think," retorted the schoolteacher. "Try Jill Madison's number, will you?"

Gertrude had to call stenographic to get the number. She dialed it, and again the results were a total blank. "Shall I keep trying?" Gertrude wanted to know. But Miss Withers didn't think that would be of any use.

She went back to her own office, sat down at the desk and stared at the funeral lilies on the wall. There were plenty of pieces in the jigsaw, but instead of fitting together they kept dividing into smaller pieces. . . .

Then there came a sharp knock on her door, and Buster Haight entered. That young man looked considerably the worse for wear this morning. If he had slept at all it was in the suit he was wearing now.

"I just had to see you, Miss Withers," he exploded. "It's about Jill——"

"I know. She didn't come to work this morning. After last night perhaps she didn't feel up to it."

"Yes, but——" He shook his head. "She didn't come home last night. I know, because on my way down this morning I stopped at her place. I sort of hoped I could buy her breakfast or something. And her porch light was still on, and the morning milk and the paper were on the step."

Miss Withers nodded. "Excellent deducting, young man. The milk and paper alone might only mean that she hadn't risen, but the porch light rather proves your point. And just what do you want me to do about it?"

Buster leaned over her desk, and, in spite of herself, Miss Withers couldn't help looking at his nails. Long and well manicured. With a transparent liquid polish too. Some men used that, but the schoolteacher disapproved. "I want you to use your influence to find her!" he demanded. "You're hand in glove with the police—everybody knows that. And she went off last night with that Dobie—you know what he is!"

"I don't see that it is any of my business——" the schoolteacher began.

"But it is! You don't suppose she'd stay out all night of her own free will! Something's happened to her!"

"You want me to report her disappearance to the police, is that it? I warn you, they won't pay much attention. People have to be missing more than a few hours before they take it seriously."

"Well, try, please!" Buster was very serious about this. Miss Withers, however, was saved the trouble. Because at that moment her telephone rang. It was the inspector, who said that he was down at headquarters in the office of the lieutenant.

"Just thought you might like to know that one of our suspects has taken it on the lam," he announced.

"I know, Oscar, I know. It's Virgil Dobie—and his secretary is likewise missing."

"Well, maybe here's something you didn't know," Piper snapped back. "The lieutenant here tried to fasten a tail on Dobie this morning, but it was too late. The guy had already hired a plane out at Glendale Airport and taken a powder."

Miss Withers had a chill feeling at the base of her spine. Yet there was something wrong about all this, something that didn't fit into the picture at all.

"Oscar, where did he take off for? I mean, aren't planes supposed to register their destination so they can be traced if they show up missing?"

"'Supposed to' is right. But this one didn't. It was a Vultee low-wing job—capable of around four hundred miles an hour wide open. So by this time Virgil Dobie could be in Canada. Anyway, the lieutenant has ordered a general alarm sent out covering all airports. We ought to hear something soon, unless they set down in a cow pasture."

Miss Withers hung up and looked at her unhappy caller. "Do you really love her so much?" she asked.

Buster shrugged. "How do I know? They say it takes two people to be in love, and it's only now and then that Jill knows I'm alive. All I know is, the girl is always in my mind. Maybe I love her, maybe I hate her. I think maybe it's both. . . ."

"You'll get over it," she promised him. "'Men have died, and worms have eaten them, but not for love. . . .'"

Buster didn't think he was likely to get over it. And when he had left Miss Hildegarde Withers shook her head sadly. She was very much afraid that young Haight would have to get over loving Jill whether he wanted to or not. A grim and unpleasant certainty began to grip her, and deep in the back of her mind a little red light began to glow. . . .

It was lunch time, but that seemed unimportant now. She took out her notes, stared at them blankly. No new light could be, at the moment, shed upon them. Then there was the list of comings and goings for this floor on the afternoon of Stafford's murder. She frowned over that for a while.

Every writer on the floor had had an opportunity to kill Saul Stafford. But that didn't preclude the possibility that some outsider had done it. There had been several callers on the floor that afternoon between the hours of three and five. A Mr Pape—that would be the insurance man. She made a small check after his name. Then Wagman, the agent. And someone with the intriguing name of Parlay Jones had asked for Dobie—several times earlier in the day too.

She went down the hall and consulted Gertrude. "I want to talk to this Mr Harry Pape," she admitted. "Do you know where I could find him?"

Gertrude knew. But nobody ever had to seek out Mr Pape. All that would be necessary would be to hint that she would let him into her office with his brief case. "Getting him out is tougher, though," the girl added. "I'll make an appointment."

With Mr Pape's call arranged for, Miss Withers turned to the other two names on her list. There was not much point in worrying about Wagman—he had lost an excellent meal ticket when Stafford died and would hardly have cut his own throat. But as for Mr Parlay Jones...

"He's easy, too," Gertrude told her. "That's the book-ie who comes around every noon taking bets, and every night to pay off. He's probaby in the studio right now. I'll check at the gate."

Ten minutes later Miss Hildegarde Withers was closeted in her office with a lean and serious young man who looked like a certified public accountant. He produced copies of the *Daily Racing Form* and scratch sheet and waited hopefully.

"So sorry," said Miss Withers. "But I only bet on the horses once, and then I bet every horse in the race to win.* I made three hundred and sixty dollars on it too. Which was a good time to quit."

---

*See *The Puzzle of the Red Stallion*. Crime Club, 1935.

Mr Jones was very mildly interested. He was not interested at all when she tried to pump him about the betting transactions of Virgil Dobie.

"Trade secrets, lady," he said. "I never talk about my clients. . . ."

"I'm afraid you'll have to talk about this one," she came back, and produced Mr Lothian's little white card. "I'm of the opinion that he would gladly bar you from the studio if I asked him."

"Lady," said Parlay Jones earnestly, "he'd bar me from the studio if he knew who I am and why I'm in it." The starch had gone out of the man. "What do you want to know?"

"I want to know the exact amount of Virgil Dobie's account with you."

He took out a small notebook, ruffled the pages and said, "Seventeen hundred and forty-two dollars—up to today, and I guess he hasn't picked any horses, because I haven't heard from him."

"You won't," said Miss Withers. "Just a minute—don't go. How much did the late Saul Stafford owe you?"

Mr Jones ruffled his notebook pages again, frowned and reported, "Exactly six hundred and fifty. Which I'll never get—not unless they pay off in hell."

"Thank you, that will be all," the schoolteacher told him stiffly. Then she noticed that he was staring down at a scrap of paper on her desk. "Where did you get hold of that?" he demanded. "I thought you didn't bet?"

She looked and saw that it was the sheet on which she had copied the cryptic lines of figures she found in Virgil Dobie's desk drawer, the one beginning, "****Pix." "Never mind where I got it—what is it?"

He almost smiled. "I call it the 'Bookies' Curse.' It's a system, lady. The god-damnedest system that ever was. Because if you play it and stick to it you can win about a hundred bucks a day, day after day."

Intrigued, Miss Withers wheedled him into explaining further. "Look, lady," he said. "That first column under the heading 'Pix'—that means the picks made by the handicapper you want to follow. In this system you never try to pick the horses yourself, but follow some good clocker like the boys in the *Racing Form* or one of the newspaper handicappers." He took the sheet, added a few words here and there.

****Pix	Code	Put	Take
1 Ajax		2	
2 Sunnyjim		2	
3 Babette		2	
1 Lady Play	2	2	$ 6.80
2 Sesenta	2	2	
3 Bump	2	2	
1 ect.	2	2	
2	8	4	
3	8	4	
1	12	6	
2	18	(8)	$54.00
3	18	8	
1	26	12	
2	2	2	
3	32	(16)	$88.40

"In the first column, under picks, you put down the horses that your handicapper selects to come first, second and third. And you bet two bucks on each to win. Suppose they all run out of the money. Then you bet the same in the next race, writing down a code number equal to your bet—two bucks. Suppose Lady Play, the first pick, wins. You write the price out in the 'Take' column.

"Now the system begins to work. In the third race

you drop back to a two-dollar bet for the first horse because that number won last time. But on the other two you figure out a new code number, which is the old code number for that position plus the money wagered on the two losing horses you had in the previous race. You only bet half your code number—which is four bucks on the second and third picks. We'll say they all run out. . . .

"So in the fourth race you have codes of twelve, eighteen and eighteen. You bet six, eight and eight because there's no nine-dollar window at the track. The second horse wins with eight on his nose, and you take fifty-four dollars. And so on and so on. See how easy it is?"

Miss Withers nodded slowly. "If I understand you correctly, this system is a sure way of making a hundred dollars a day?"

He shrugged. "Pretty near that. Of course, you have to make some big bets—up to thirty-six dollars a race, and sometimes more. It's not so easy to stick to a system. You see everybody else betting on the favorite and you know he'll win and you hate to put all that dough on a horse that hasn't a chance. But if you stick to this system you'll do pretty good." He nodded. "So much so that I'll give you fifty bucks to tear up that sheet of paper. If it gets around the studio I'm a ruined bookie."

"Thank you, but I'll keep it," Miss Withers told him. "I will also promise you not to play it, either with you or any other bookie."* She folded up the slip of paper and put it carefully away. Where it fitted into her puzzle she could not at the moment imagine, but one never knew.

Mr Parlay Jones was growing very restless, but she had one question more. "When a client of yours gets behind and owes you a lot of money just what steps do you take to collect?"

He hesitated. "Steps? Oh, you mean, do we turn on the heat?" He shook his head. "It's funny about that, but

---

*N.B. All the same, Miss Withers followed it for the last week of the 1940 race meeting at Santa Anita, using the picks of Mr Oscar Otis of the Los Angeles *Times*, and had (paper) profits of $1675. *Verb. sap.*

we never lose much, unless somebody dies like this guy Stafford. People will let their dentist and doctor go hungry, they'll stall the department stores and the landlord, but they'll almost always pay up on a gambling debt. Especially to a bookie, because they want to keep betting with him. See?"

Miss Withers finally parted company with Mr Parlay Jones and was immediately advised that a Mr Pape was outside to see her.

He turned out to be an effervescent and youngish man in gray-green tweeds, and at the expense of taking out a small annuity policy which she probably needed anyhow, she learned that Mr Pape had written straight life policies for both Saul Stafford and Virgil Dobie to the amount of five thousand dollars, naming each other as beneficiary. "I do that for a number of writing teams in the business," he explained. "It's fine protection for them in case something happens. . . ."

"As it did in the case of Mr Stafford?" she inquired.

Pape shrugged. "Too bad about that. He let his policy lapse. If he'd kept up the payments Virgil Dobie would collect five thousand dollars. There's a lesson for all of us—never let your insurance lapse."

Miss Withers doubted if Saul Stafford was uneasy in his grave—or on his marble slab—because of the fact that his former collaborator was not to collect five thousand dollars but she did not say so.

When Mr Pape took his departure she made a number of neat notations on a sheet of paper. The case was winding up—she could see that. Only there were still so many, so very many, loose ends.

She called up the inspector, advised him that Virgil Dobie owed his bookie $1742, and that he had expected to collect five thousand from the policy carried by Saul Stafford.

"That's good enough for me," Piper told her. "I'm sticking right here with the lieutenant, and we'll soon track the guy down. They just wired that the plane stopped at an airport fifty miles this side of Albuquerque.

To gas up, I suppose. But it took off again before anybody could pick 'em up."

"Oscar, did anybody report a girl's being on that plane?"

The inspector didn't think so. And therefore Miss Hildegarde Withers' grim certainty became more certain than ever.

Something had happened to Jill Madison.

It was a bitter pill for Miss Withers to take. Sleuthing was fun, right enough, but she had no patience with detectives who let people go on being murdered under their very noses. She might have seen the light earlier—she might have prevented this last tragedy.

That was water over the dam anyway. "Oscar," she said into the telephone, "I want you to meet me as quick as ever you can get there at Jill Madison's apartment. What? No, she won't be there. Never mind how I know."

The place turned out to be a small, neat apartment house with yellow shutters, located on a side street between Beverly Hills and Hollywood. Oscar Piper arrived just at the moment when Miss Withers had identified the separate entrance of Jill's apartment by its folded *Examiner*, the bottle of Grade A on the stoop and the feeble electric light burning over the door.

"The first thing the police do when anybody disappears or is murdered is to search their apartment," she told the inspector. "I wanted to beat them to it. Now all we have to do is to get in. . . ."

She made tentative experiments with a hairpin, but the lock was modern. She looked under the door mat, beneath a flower pot and on top of the doorjamb, but found no key cached there. And there was really no satisfactory excuse that they could give to the manager of the place.

"Unless you could flash your badge," Miss Withers suggested hopefully. But that fell through, too, because there was no resident manager here.

"I'd better go back downtown and get the lieutenant

and some skeleton keys and a search warrant," the inspector said. "Or, better still, we could drop the whole thing and——"

"Eureka!" cried the schoolteacher happily, discovering that the side window was partially open. It was easy enough to pry through the screen, raise the window higher. . . .

They were finally inside, standing in the middle of a little living room crowded with books and furniture and ash trays. Even the goldfish bowl was crowded with weird, goggling fish.

Into the bedroom—in which quite evidently someone had dressed in a hurry. Two evening dresses had been tried and found wanting, left lying on the bed. Several pairs of dance sandals lay scattered about, a costume-jewelry bracelet hung on the bedpost and a faint film of powder floated in the air.

"Just what in blazes are we looking for?" the inspector demanded unhappily.

"I'll know it when I find it," Miss Withers said grimly. And then they heard the sound of a key in the front door. It opened, and Virgil Dobie stood in the doorway, as surprised as they.

For a moment time stood still. Then: "You're under arrest," Oscar Piper greeted him. "Come clean, what did you do with her body?"

Dobie's thick eyebrows went up almost to his hairline. "*What* body?"

"Jill Madison's, of course!" cut in Miss Withers.

"Nothing, yet," said Virgil Dobie seriously. "But I was just going to carry it across the threshold. Tradition and good luck and all that. . . ."

They realized, a bit late, that Jill stood behind him—Jill Madison, alive and well and covered with orchids.

"We flew to New Mexico," Dobie began to explain. "Is that any reason for——?"

"You can be the first to congratulate us!" Jill greeted them, her voice faintly shrill and strained. "We're married!"

and wine-dark-whiskers and a stern woman, the Inspector . . . Oh, I beg your pardon — I meant to say

XI

The Tale must be **ABOUT DEAD BODIES,**
Or very wicked people, preferably both....

DOROTHY SAYERS

Both Mr and Mrs Dobie wore the dazed and brittle look which passes for ecstatic happiness among newly married couples. "We were married by a justice of the peace in Mesa City at nine o'clock this morning," the groom informed their uninvited callers. "Then we climbed right back into the plane."

"Congratulations, I'm sure," offered Miss Withers. Her mind was going around and around. The entire jigsaw was stirred up as if some mad simian had swung down by his tail and maliciously mangled it into *pi*. "I should hate to confess to you the suspicions that we've been sharing. After what's been happening——"

Virgil Dobie said he understood. "Maybe you think this isn't just the proper and fitting time to get married?" He put his arm around the bride. "Well, it seemed to me that Jill might possibly need a little protection. With people getting murdered all around her . . ."

The inspector nodded. "*We* had no business busting in here in the first place, and I guess we'd better be going now. Come on, Hildegarde, let's find another tree to bark up."

159

"Just a minute," said the schoolteacher absently. "I don't——" Then she whirled on Virgil Dobie. "Young man, would you mind answering two or three questions for me?"

"Why—that depends on what they are."

"Here goes," said the schoolteacher. "First, just how much money do you owe your bookie, Mr Parlay Jones?"

"Not a dime. Next question?"

"Aha!" cried Miss Withers. "You'll be surprised to know, young man, that I had a talk with him this morning and that he said your account was seventeen hundred and something——"

"It is," Virgil Dobie assured her. "Only he owes it to me. I've been beating him about a hundred bucks a day, and it's piled up."

"You know, Hildegarde," put in the inspector, "sometimes bookies *do* owe people."

"Tell it to Ripley," she snapped. "But, Mr. Dobie, isn't it true that Saul Stafford was in debt to the bookie?"

"Sure he was," said Dobie. "He didn't have the system I use. Saul tried to pick horses on form and because he liked the color of their eyes. I've got a system that's as good as an annuity any day. When I get tired of Hollywood I'm going to take my system and try it at every track in America. Pittsburgh Phil the Second——"

"But Saul Stafford never used your system?" she went on.

"No, and that's why he died owing his bookie."

"Of course, if you wanted to be nice you could pay off Saul Stafford's account with Parlay Jones, using the insurance money that you are going to get as beneficiary!"

Virgil Dobie blinked. "Insurance money? Oh, you mean Saul's policy?" He shook his head. "That would be a nice idea, only there isn't any insurance money. Saul let his policy lapse months ago."

"You knew that? When did you find it out?"

"At the time, of course. Harry Pape wrote me about it, not wanting to lose an account. He thought maybe I could talk Saul into keeping up the premiums, but I couldn't."

"If you're quite through," Jill began desperately, "I——"

But Miss Withers wasn't. "Just one question more, and then we'll leave you two lovebirds alone. I just want to ask you, Mr Dobie—*who is Derek Laval?*"

There was a short pause. "Laval? Why, everybody knows him. He's at every cocktail party and première in town. Sort of Hollywood fixture, like Prince Mike Romanoff or Sy Bartlett or . . ."

"Or George Spelvin?" said Miss Withers softly.

It was almost a full minute before Virgil Dobie remembered to take a breath. But the expression which came over his face was almost one of relief.

"Yes, like George Spelvin," he admitted.

The inspector looked so blank and bewildered at this point that Miss Withers turned to him. "George Spelvin, the well-known actor," she reminded him. He nodded, vaguely remembering the name.

"Thank you both so much," Miss Withers was saying briskly. "I'm sorry we interrupted you, and I hope you'll forgive us for housebreaking. But there have been several murders, and I think it would be awfully nice if there weren't any more."

She was about to herd the inspector out of the place, but Jill would have none of that. "Please!" she cried. "This isn't just an ordinary day. It's supposed to be a happy day, a celebration. Won't you drink a toast with us—please?"

Swiftly from the tiny, crowded kitchenette she produced a small bottle and four glasses. "It ought to be champagne," she explained. "But this will have to do—it's California brandy."

The inspector accepted his glass somewhat reluctantly, feeling that he was inside this apartment under somewhat false colors. Miss Withers also shied off somewhat from the idea of drinking even this small thimbleful of spirits.

But it was a wedding day. "Er—to the bride!" she managed, and then took a tentative sip of the fire water.

The inspector was equally conservative. Only Jill Madison—now Jill Dobie—did full justice to the toast. For the groom barely wet his lips.

"I'm sorry," said Virgil Dobie when he saw that they were all looking at him. "But I just made a resolution. I'm on the wagon, for good and all. I've seen too much of what effect this sauce—I mean alcohol—has on people. Look what it did for Saul Stafford. Two drinks, and he'd talk your arm off. And I have an idea he'd be alive and with us today if he hadn't hit the bottle."

Jill stared at her husband, extremely amazed. "But—but that's *wonderful!* If you really mean. . . ."

Virgil Dobie really meant it. "I'm a new man," he informed them. "Watch me. Eight hours' sleep a night, up bright and early and to the studio by nine o'clock, no more gags, plenty of yeses for Mr Nincom. . . ."

"Speaking of Mr Nincom," Miss Withers put in, "he feels very strongly about your disappearance today. In fact, he seemed to infer that you were fired. Shouldn't you telephone him or something?"

"Wait!" Jill interrupted. "I know that man better than any of you. There's still time enough. It would be better if we walked in on him. The happy couple and so forth—he couldn't resist being nice about the whole thing."

Virgil Dobie saw reason in that. "And another thing—he can't fire me for staying away if I show up, even at quarter of five. We'll report for work. And on the way in we'll stop at Wardrobe and borrow a veil and some prop flowers for you!"

So that is the way it happened. The inspector begged off, feeling that he didn't quite belong. But Miss Withers, practically playing the unaccustomed part of flower girl and twelve bridesmaids, marched into Mr Thorwald L. Nincom's story conference, followed by a blushing bride and groom.

For the rest of that day the ancient tragedy of poor Lizzie Bordon was forgotten in this modern surprise romance between the loveliest secretary and the maddest hooligan writer in Hollywood.

Jill's premise had been right. Mr Nincom slipped at once into the role of the crusty but warmhearted employer and played it for all he was worth. He grabbed up the telephone, ordered champagne from the nearest restaurant and cameras from Publicity.

The popping of corks drew Mammoth employees by the dozens into the Nincom offices. Writers, directors, secretaries, messengers, props, grips and cameramen. . . .

The bride was toasted so many times that it appeared that she would be "brown on both sides," as Doug August put it. Miss Withers watched the party develop, watched Virgil Dobie as he accepted glass after glass and put them quietly down for someone else to empty. . . .

Melicent Manning was sobbing quietly in a corner. Frankie Firsk had his arm about Virgil Dobie's shoulder and was making a speech, interlarded with quotations from the minor modern poets.

Wilfred Josef had just one glass of wine and then headed for the door where Miss Withers halted him. "What are you going to give the happy couple for a wedding present?" she asked.

"I haven't the slightest idea," Mr Josef said. His hand went instinctively to his beard, jerked away as he felt the charred remnants. "But here's a limerick for you. There was a young lady named Jill, Who went after a man with a will. She sat down beside him and roped him and tied him, But I hate to be in at the kill."

He nodded, smiled and was gone.

Willy Abend had started a crap game in the corner behind Mr Nincom's desk and was doing rather well at it. And then Mr Nincom produced his baton from the desk and rapped with it for silence.

"Ladies and gentlemen—and friends!" he began. "It is my great pleasure on this happy occasion to announce my wedding present to the bride. During the last two months my whole unit has been going mad in an attempt

to find the perfect person to play the part of Miss Lizzie
Borden. Well, a great idea just came to me. Why should
we look so far afield, why should we test every New York
actress, every Hollywood star, when we have an opportunity of finding and developing real talent right here and
now?—talent from this very office."

Everybody hushed, wondering. . . . Mr Nincom drained
his glass. "I want to announce that I intend to test Miss Jill
Madison—the present Mrs. Virgil Dobie—for the part of
Lizzie Borden!"

Jill, who was at the moment standing on a desk with a
glass of bubbling wine in either hand, tried to say something. But Mr Nincom was in the groove.

"Right here in this room," he continued, "we have
the director, we have the stage crew—and there is no
reason why we can't costume Mrs Dobie, give her a scene
to read and take the test over on one of the stages right
now. And if it comes out well we'll plaster the nation with
announcements tomorrow morning!"

There were cheers. "Thank you," said Mr Nincom. "I
guess if Dave Selznick can get an unknown actress to play
Scarlett, I can pull Jill out of the hat to play Lizzie. A last
toast—good luck to Thorwald L. Nincom's new discovery—
and then we'll make a test such as never was made
before!"

There were tremendous cheers, and the party broke
up.

Miss Hildegarde Withers seized upon Buster Haight
outside in the studio street, a young man lost and unhappy
and vaguely distressed. "Come, come!" she said. "'False
though she be to me and love, I'll ne'er pursue revenge;
for still the charmer I approve, Though I deplore her
change. . . .'"

"This is no time for Congrève," said Buster. "He's as
outdated as Confucius."

"What are you going to do?" she wanted to know.

"I don't know," said Buster. There was a wild and
reckless expression around his young mouth, and his eyes

had lost their color. "I'm supposed to be out here learning the picture business. Well, I guess I'm learning it the hard way."

He turned and rushed off into the night, leaving Miss Withers shaking her head. She had dealt successfully with many ills, but youth was one which had no panacea.

The schoolteacher turned toward the Writers' Building, sought her own office and sat down at her desk. Everything was just the same. The gas radiator leered at her from the corner, daring her to turn it on again. On the wall the photograph of the tired calla lilies struck a funeral note. . . .

She picked up the phone, managed to get a night line before Gertrude closed up and went home. There was a great deal to do, and Miss Withers was afraid that it was too late to do it.

But she made certain calls anyhow.

After a while she heard someone come down the hall. A light burned in Virgil Dobie's office.

"Oh, hello," he said, when she burst in.

"What's the matter, Mr Dobie, did you get tired of the celebration?"

He nodded. "They're all over on the test stage, making shots of Jill. Honestly, do you think she could play Lizzie Borden?"

"Anything can happen in Hollywood," said Miss Withers. "If I remember correctly, one of our biggest stars was jerking soda when she was discovered, and another was manicuring fingernails."

It was at that moment that a messenger boy brought in a package wrapped as a gift. "For Mr and Mrs Virgil Dobie." It turned out to be a thousand aspirin tablets in a large bottle. "With the best wishes of Wilfred Josef," was the card.

So Josef had decided upon a wedding present after all. "At least it's something we can use," Dobie said.

Miss Withers nodded. "A very useful present. You've been looking a bit headachy all day."

She brought a glass of water, watched while Virgil Dobie tossed off three pellets. "If you don't mind, I'll borrow a couple of them myself," she said, and did. "I'll take them later," added Miss Withers.

But it was only ten minutes later when she burst back into Virgil Dobie's office, her face white as a sheet. She faced the man, her hands trembling.

"Those pills!" she cried. "They——I mean——"

"What, the aspirin?"

"I just started to take one—and they're *not* aspirin! Didn't you notice the bitter taste? Well, you should have. I should have guessed when they came from Wilfred Josef, the man to whom your prank gave a lifelong phobia. He cannot even light a cigarette because of the joke you pulled on him—no wonder he gave you this kind of wedding present!"

Dobbie stared at her blankly.

"It's *poison!*" cried Miss Withers. "Arsenic, I think. I spat it out. Don't you notice anything?"

Virgil Dobie sank back in his chair. "Poison? Oh, come, come. Josef wouldn't do that——"

"Wouldn't he! Practical jokers always run into somebody who won't take the joke if they keep on long enough. And you took *three* of those pills——"

"But I had a headache!" Dobie protested. "I didn't imagine——"

"So had I! Neither did I!"

They stared at each other for a moment, and then Miss Withers snatched up the telephone. "Don't you worry!" she said. "There is plenty of time. Hello? I want the studio infirmary. Yes. Yes? Doctor Evenson? Can you get over here right away?—and bring a stomach pump?"

Virgil Dobie didn't believe it. He couldn't believe that anybody would try to murder him—not just because of a practical joke that he had played days ago. . . .

But he leaned back on the couch in his office, a grayish-green look on is face. And after a few moments Dr

Evenson arrived, nodded at Miss Withers and started to open his instrument case.

"I'll wait outside," said the schoolteacher.

It was nearly half an hour later when Dr Evenson emerged. He seemed very pleased with himself. "Everything will be okay," he told Miss Withers. "The man is in fine shape."

"You've been wonderful, Doctor," she assured him. Then she went back into the office.

Virgil Dobie lay on the couch, and his face was a pale puce color now. But he lifted his hand feebly. "Don' tell Jill . . ." he managed. "Worry her. No good. I'm okay. . . ."

"Of course you're okay," said the schoolteacher. "You're fine."

"That stomach-pump thing," he said loudly, "that's a terrible thing to go through. Almost rather die from poison, eh? Sure—I'd rather die from poison. . . ."

"You won't die from anything," she advised him. "Because I was right here on the spot. Now just relax, Mr Dobie. I'll keep this from your wife until you feel better. She's very busy at the moment over on the test stage, so she'll never know. . . ."

"Thanks," said Virgil Dobie fervently. "You're a swell guy. A fellow can really talk to you. . . ."

His speech was louder now, and he seemed to have trouble with his consonants. "Yes sir, some women understand men, and you're one of them. . . ."

"Thank you," said Miss Hildegarde Withers. "I understand about headaches, too, because I have one." She rubbed her forehead.

"Sure," Virgil Dobie said. "All intellectual people have headaches. I have 'em at the drop of a hat. Sign of brains. . . ."

"Thank you," Miss Withers told him. "Do you suppose that George Spelvin has headaches?"

Dobie frowned. "Spelvin? Oh yes. You know about that, don't you? Guess there's no use trying to fool you."

"Not much," confessed Miss Withers.

"Well, why not?" he went on, his voice loud and stumbling and insistent. "This income-tax thing is terrific. Out here in pictures we make big salaries for a few years, five or ten at the most, but Uncle Sam wants the same percentage as he'd take from any stockbroker who has a sure thing for life. You can't blame us for trying to dodge——"

"Dodge? Just what do you mean?"

"Why, the way I did. I lent a lot of money to Derek Laval—only there isn't any such guy—and charged it off to a loss. So did Saul; so do lots of guys. Derek Laval is a phony, a nom de plume. Whenever any of the boys gets into a hell of a jam he gives that name, whether it's a traffic ticket, a girl, or what?"

"Of course," chimed in Miss Withers. "Whether he is arrested for speeding or held for being in a raided night spot or playing polo against the rules laid down by the studio. . . ."

Dobie nodded again. "That must have been Doug August playing polo. He's not the only one to take a phony name. Spence Tracy usually has to play under the name of Murphy when he's making a picture because Metro don't like the idea of his risking that million-dollar face. As for the rest of the boys, anybody in Hollywood is likely to give the name of Derek Laval when he gets in a jam. It's like the actors—when they have to play two parts in one play they take the name of George Spelvin for the minor part."

He frowned and tried to sit up. "Say, why am I talking your arm off like this?"

Miss Withers smiled. "But, of course, Mr Dobie. You have every reason to co-operate with me. After all, the murderer is a menace to each and every one of us until he is caught."

"That's right," Dobie admitted, still speaking a bit thickly.

"He killed your collaborator and best friend in cold blood. He tried to kill me because I was snooping too close and he succeeded in doing away with a studio driver and a girl hitchhiker. And he killed Lillian Gissing. . . ."

"Yeah. And to top it all off he just tried to kill me!"

Miss Withers hesitated. "Yes, *didn't* he? But don't worry about that. Doctor Evenson got it out of you before it could do you any real harm." She smiled. "You feel better, don't you?"

Dobie decided that he did. "My headache is better anyway," he said. "Nothing like a dose of arsenic to cure a bad case of migraine, what?" He shook his head as if to clear it from cobwebs. "Say, wait a minute, doesn't this solve the whole case? Why don't you call in the police and have them arrest Wilfred Josef?"

"For several reasons," said Miss Hildegarde Withers. "And the most important one is that it just occurred to me that the handwriting on the note attached to that aspirin bottle isn't Wilfred Josef's at all!"

"What? But—but whose is it then?"

"I haven't the slightest idea," lied Miss Hildegarde Withers. "But during my investigations I've managed to collect samples of the handwriting of most of the characters involved in this case. I think if you don't mind I'll borrow that card and start making some comparisons. . . ."

"Go ahead," muttered Virgil Dobie. "Things are moving too fast for me. I'll just lie here and let things stop whirling around in my head. . . ."

She started to leave, and he started up. "Oh, before I forget," he called after her. "Thanks for saving my life."

Miss Withers took a bow and then went back to her own office. Things were not working out quite as she had hoped. She felt very much out of her element, very much alone and bewildered. . . .

And the least of her problems was the matter of who had written the note attached to the bottle of aspirin tablets. She had taken a desperate chance, had played her ace in the hole. And it had come to nothing.

She couldn't take this case to the police. She couldn't even take it to the inspector. It was woven all of moonbeams, gossamer thin. . . .

She called Mr Nincom's office, but there was no

answer. The great man must still be superintending the screen test which was his wedding present to the luscious Jill.

She called Chief Sansom, but he seemed to be out. "When he comes back I'll have him check with you," was the best information she could get. And finally she called the inspector, both at his hotel and at downtown headquarters. Another blank. . . .

"Just tell him it's a '4-11' in Miss Withers's office," she left the message. That meant "riot call" in police code.

She sat there for half an hour, made little meaningless diagrams on sheets of paper. And then finally there came a knock on her door. It was Virgil Dobie, his hair dark as if it had been recently drenched with water.

"Any luck?" he wanted to know, swaying unsteadily.

"Not in the slightest," she advised him.

He came over to the desk, peered at her scribblings. "You can't figure out who wrote that note?"

"No," she lied. "I can't. But that's only one of my headaches. . . ."

"Speaking of headaches," said Virgil Dobie pleasantly, "I know a wonderful remedy."

"Not *aspirin!*" she said quickly.

"No, no drugs at all. It's a knack I happen to have. You've heard about some people rubbing headaches away?"

She thought that she had heard about that. A combination of the ancient idea of laying on hands and of the powers of massage.

"I can do it," Virgil Dobie said, nodding.

"Thank you so much, but I don't know—my head seems better," she hedged. "Yes, much better. . . ."

"Just lean back and relax," Virgil Dobie said. He came closer, swaying slightly on his feet, though his eyes were clear now. "I'll fix that headache of yours. It's a small enough return for what you've done for me today. . . ."

Powerless to move, she sat there in her chair as Dobie bent over her. "You have to relax completely," he said. And his hand started to stroke her forehead, the long fingers moving upward from the bridge of her nose toward the hairline.

Then the other hand touched her, pressing gently on her sinuses, against the subtle places near eyes and under nostrils and in front of the ears, relaxing her muscles. . . .

"Just sink back," said Virgil Dobie. His voice was very soft, very far away. . . .

His fingers closed on her temples, pressing deep into the curve just back of her brows. . . .

"That's a funny thing about Hollywood," Dobie was saying in a soft and almost caressing voice. "The tempo of life is speeded up; everything is so hectic and rushing that we all get headaches. Sometimes we make our own headaches. Sometimes we're shackled to our headaches, the way I was shackled to Saul Stafford."

His hands were strong and caressing and very swift now. "You see, Saul was like an 'Old Man of the Sea' to me. We were typed as a team, typed forever and ever. I could never get a job without him. I could never get away from him. I didn't need the work—I have a race system that I think will make me a million dollars. And if it doesn't it's fun trying it. But Saul clung to me. He couldn't drive a car; he couldn't do anything. He hung on to me. If I cast him off I was set down as a heel. . . ."

"My headache is all cured," Miss Withers muttered.

But Virgil Dobie wasn't listening. "Funny thing about Saul," he went on. "He couldn't drink. When he drank he talked. He talked about a lot of things, but mostly about something that happened years and years ago back in New York. He found out how to commit a murder an easy, perfect way. It worked, and Saul was smart enough not ever to try it again. . . ."

She tried to sit up, but Virgil Dobie's hands held her there. "That was a mistake on Saul's part. Because you never should talk too much. I'm never going to talk too much. Well, maybe right now, because I can't help it. But not tomorrow. . . .

"I don't know why I'm talking now. Heaven knows I

didn't intend to. I hadn't the slightest idea of telling anybody what I'm telling you. But with you it doesn't matter. . . . You see, ever since Saul and I have been working together he's had the original ideas and I've put them into final form. I can take any of Saul's ideas and work them up into something. So why not take his idea of murder, eh? Of course. Nothing to it. . . ."

Miss Withers began to struggle, but it was a bit late. Because Virgil Dobie's right hand was across her forehead, the fingers clamped down on her cheek. And the left hand was on the back of her head, giving a terrific leverage. . . .

She drew a quick breath, tried to tense the muscles of her neck to resist the terrible pressure that was swinging her head around in an impossible circle. . . .

In the midst of her agony, in the midst of her terror, there was a cry of exaltation. For this was how the murders had been committed. This was the answer to all her questions. . . .

There was strange noises, a sound of roaring in Miss Hildegarde Withers' ears, and then silence.

XII

It does not want to beat any more,
And why should it beat?
This is the end of the journey;
THE THING IS FOUND....

CHARLOTTE MEW

"Easy does it," came the inspector's voice. Someone was dabbing water in Miss Withers' face, a sensation that she disliked extremely.

"I'm perfectly all right," she insisted, and sat up.

She was on the couch in her own office. "Sure you're all right," the inspector was saying a bit dubiously. "Of course."

She frowned at him. "Oscar!"

"Yes?"

"How did you manage to arrive just in the nick of time?"

"Well, if you must know, I didn't. We were out in the hall for ten minutes or so, listening through the door to your chat with Mr Dobie. He was talking so well that we hated to interrupt."

"Well, you certainly waited until the last minute," she snapped. "He was actually starting to wring my neck when you came in. Where is he, by the way?"

173

"The lieutenant and Sansom carted him away," Oscar Piper admitted. "I hope you don't mind?"

"The farther they took him the better I'll like it," said Miss Hildegarde Withers fervently. "I've had just about as much of Mr Virgil Dobie as I can stand."

"I see what you mean," said the inspector. "But just to keep the record clear I hope you won't mind clarifying a few points. I understand why Virgil Dobie killed Stafford. That's obvious enough. Stafford got drunk and confessed to him how he'd got rid of Emily Harris back in New York. The perfect murder and all that. So Dobie saw the humor of turning the tables on his collaborator. . . ."

"Exactly, Oscar. Virgil Dobie wasn't a creator but he was exceptionally good at taking other people's ideas and developing them."

"Okay, okay. And I understand about his twisting necks when he could get the victim to relax—in Stafford's case he was supposed to be rubbing away a headache and in the Lillian Gissing job he probably found her passed out. But what I don't see is, how did he have *time* to murder Stafford? Was the girl lying when she said she talked to Stafford on the phone after Virgil Dobie left the floor?"

Miss Withers shook her head. "Dobie saw to it that she called Stafford. It was all part of his alibi. He was checked out by that time. But if the woman who sells neckties could sneak through by walking on her hands and knees, why couldn't Virgil Dobie? He came up on the floor to fill his tobacco pouch, learned that Saul Stafford was getting wise to things and was planning on calling in a detective—so he checked out only to crawl back and murder the man!"

"It could be," Piper admitted. "But from there on . . ."

"From there on everything went smoothly. Until Mr Dobie discovered that I was close on his trail. He tried to built up the imaginary character of Derek Laval for a scapegoat. But I got too close to him. That was why he took very special steps to make sure that I wouldn't survive the trip up to Arrowhead. The studio cars are kept in a garage at the back of this lot, Oscar, and anybody could have access to them. That time he struck down two innocent people but missed me."

"And what about Lillian?"

"He had to kill her, Oscar. There wasn't any choice by that time. Because, as his secretary, Lillian knew where to look for the canceled checks. You know, the checks that Dobie had made out to an imaginary character, Derek Laval, in order to whittle down his income tax."

"But why Laval?"

"It was just a name, Oscar. Stafford used it in New York, and later when he came out here all the boys started to use it. Whenever any of them got into a jam or wanted to play fast and loose with a girl they stepped into the character of Derek Laval. They signed it to hotel registers, to ribald poetry, to anything. . . ."

"Like George Spelvin?"

"Exactly. But you see, the most vulnerable point for Virgil Dobie was that he had written those checks—the ones I almost caught Lillian abstracting from his office. She lied and said she couldn't find them, but that was only because she hoped to make something of them later. It was at Shapiro's that she finally got up nerve enough to approach Virgil Dobie and try a bit of polite blackmail, and it was her hard luck that just then the lights went out. She was halfseas over anyway, and Dobie couldn't resist giving her the same treatment he had given Stafford. Afterward he carried her body downstairs and tried to make it look as if she had fallen.

"You see, Oscar, Dobie thought he was safe because of his alibi and because he had nothing to gain—nothing directly, that is—from Saul Stafford's death. He knew that the insurance policy was outlawed. He knew that without Stafford his writing career might be ended. Of course he didn't care about that because he had a system for betting the races that he was sure would keep him in luxury the rest of his days and he wanted with all his heart to be rid of Saul Stafford.

"He took another man's idea and developed it wholesale. Stafford killed Emily Harris by snapping her neck while he was supposed to be treating her headache—and it was to clever an idea to drop there. Saul Stafford made the fatal mistake of confiding it to his collaborator while in his cups, and that was the beginning of the end."

"Well," said the inspector, "I can take the Harris case out of the 'Open' file anyway. But I want to know just one more thing. How did you get Dobie to open up and talk so freely? Up to now he's been a clam, and all of a sudden you trick him into spilling his life history——"

Miss Withers showed him the little white card which had been supplied to her by Mr Lothian. "I had to use this," she explained. "I arranged for the delivery of that big bottle of aspirin, writing the card myself. Virgil Dobie had a guilty conscience about Josef and he would be likely to believe that the man tried to take some sort of revenge. Then after the aspirin I arranged for the arrival of Doctor Evenson and his stomach pump——"

"All right, all right," cut in the inspector. "But I don't see what good the stomach pump would be——"

"This one was," Miss Withers advised him. "Because there was no question of pumping Dobie's stomach at all. That was only aspirin that he took. Doctor Evenson put up quite an argument, but the little white card did its work. You see, Virgil Dobie was very insistent upon not drinking. For fear, quite obviously, that he would get liquored up and talk and give the whole show away. He probably remembered how Saul Stafford talked to him while in his cups. Anyway, I took a cue from a book I read recently—the memoirs of Doctor Joe Catton, chief consulting psychiatrist at Stanford. He tells of how he trapped a malingering killer by giving the man a nasal feeding of eight ounces of scotch whisky and thus breaking down his reserves.

"It occurred to me, Oscar, that a stomach pump might serve the same purpose. Instead of being used as planned, it served to introduce ten ounces of neat alcohol into the stomach of Virgil Dobie. Which is why he talked so freely—and why he made the tremendous mistake of trying to repeat his perfect murder with me as the victim!"

The inspector was suddenly hilarious. "Hildegarde! You mean to tell me that you got the poor guy swached on ten ounces of alcohol that he never even tasted on the way down?"

She nodded. "Perhaps it wasn't quite fair. But it was the only way to break down his reserves and make him talk."

"Talk? Virgil Dobie is so swozzled that his hangover will last him until he gets into the lethal chamber. He'll probably go down in history as the only killer who was ever booked while singing 'Down in the Lehigh Valley' at the top of his voice." Piper shook his head. "Serves him right. But all this is going to be pretty tough on that cute little wife of his. . . ."

"Good heavens, yes!"

Miss Withers leaped to her feet, and they set out in search of Jill. "The poor child must be in need of comfort if anybody ever was. . . ."

They hurried out of the Writers' Building, down the narrow and deserted studio streets to the test stage. It was empty, unlighted.

On to Mr Nincom's offices where the mouselike Miss Smythe was busily typing in the outer office. "You can go right in," she said.

Thorwald L. Nincom sat alone in his palatial office, his heavy head resting on his arm. His eyes were alight with inspiration. . . .

"What a Lizzie Borden!" he breathed softly toward the ceiling. "What power, what fire!"

"You mean the test of Jill came out satisfactorily?" asked Miss Withers, at once surprised and relieved.

"Huh?" With difficulty Mr Nincom brought his thoughts back to earth. "Oh no. Impossible, of course. The girl doesn't photograph at all. And she can't act. Froze up like a clam when they turned the lights on her. I knew it all the time. . . ."

"But how can you tell before you see the film run off?" Miss Withers demanded.

"Film? You don't think we waste film in a courtesy test like that, do you? We gave Jill her screen test with an empty camera, of course. She's just as happy——"

"Happy?" broke in Miss Withers. "Hasn't anybody told her about her husband?"

"Oh, that!" said Mr Nincom. "Yes, I believe they did. She won't have any trouble in getting an annulment under the circumstances. I don't believe she'll take it very hard. . . ."

"But where *is* she?" demanded the schoolteacher.

Mr Nincom frowned. "Jill? Oh, I believe that one of the messenger boys is taking her home. Young Haight. . . ."

"That's Buster," Miss Withers explained to the inspector.

Mr Nincom nodded. "Nice boy. A real future in this business. His father is J. Winston Haight, you know, who owns all the preferred stock of the studio."

"When your little friend Jill finds that out," the inspector said softly, "her broken heart will mend itself pronto. Well, Hildegarde, you're going to get your happy ending after all. . . ."

Miss Withers wasn't feeling particularly happy at the moment. What she wanted was a nice, quiet padded cell somewhere. . . .

"What a Lizzie Borden," Mr Nincom was repeating softly to himself. "What an actress! A bit young, perhaps, but we can fix that." He turned to his callers. "Think of it! Think of the headlines! *Shirley Temple* makes her comeback in the role of Lizzie Borden!" He sighed. "It's a box-office natural!"

Miss Hildegarde Withers closed her eyes and slumped quietly into her chair.

"Overtired, eh?" said Mr Nincom sympathetically. "You'd better take her home. I'll have my secretary call you a taxi."

The taxicab roared up to the studio gates just as

taxicabs do in the movies and stopped with a screech of brakes. "Where d'you want to go?" the driver demanded when his passengers were safely inside.

"Times Square," said the inspector fervently.

Dear Mystery Maven,

Satisfy your taste for the murderously mysterious, indulge your urge to unravel the most baffling puzzle, revel in intrigue and suspense, find out who *really* done it! Subscribe now to **The Bantam Deadline**, Bantam's new Mystery Newsletter—published quarterly and mailed to you—FREE OF CHARGE.

Take a peek behind the mask of your favorite Mystery Maker in revealing Author Profiles. Get the inside dope on mysterious pleasures to come with the publication of titles ranging from classicly delicious Murders Most British, to the finest and hardest-boiled All-Americans. And—be the first to hear about Special Mystery Offers—Contests, Fabulous Prizes (including a Mystery Tour to England), and other *very* mysterious doings!

Send in your coupon now—if you think you can bear the suspense!

□ 25789-7 **JUST ANOTHER DAY IN PARADISE,**
Maxwell $2.95

Fiddler has more money than he knows what to do with, he's tried about everything he'd ever thought of trying and there's not much left that interests him. So, when his ex-wife's twin brother disappears, when the feds begin to investigate the high-tech computer company the twin owns, and when Fiddler finds himself holding an envelope of Russian-cut diamonds, he decides to get involved. Is his ex-wife's twin selling high-tech information to the Russians?

□ 25809-5 **THE UNORTHODOX MURDER OF RABBI WAHL,** Telushkin $2.95

Rabbi Daniel Winter, the young host of the radio talk show "Religion and You," invites three guests to discuss "Feminism and Religion." He certainly expects that the three women, including Rabbi Myra Wahl, are likely to generate some sparks . . . What he doesn't expect is murder.

□ 25717-X **THE BACK-DOOR MAN,** Kantner $2.95

Ben Perkins doesn't look for trouble, but he isn't the kind of guy who looks the other way when something comes along to spark his interest. In this case, it's a wealthy widow who's a victim of embezzlement and the gold American Express card she gives him for expenses. Ben thinks it should be fun; the other people after the missing money are out to change his mind.

□ 26061-8 **"B" IS FOR BURGLAR,** Grafton $3.50

"Kinsey is a refreshing heroine."—*Washington Post Book World*

"Kinsey Millhone . . . is a stand-out specimen of the new female operatives." —*Philadelphia Inquirer*

[Millhone is] "a tough cookie with a soft center, a gregarious loner." —*Newsweek*

What appears to be a routine missing persons case for private detective Kinsey Millhone turns into a dark tangle of arson, theft and murder.

Look for them at your bookstore or use the coupon below:

BANTAM
SHOP-AT-HOME
C·A·T·A·L·O·G

Special Offer
Buy a Bantam Book
for only 50¢.

Now you can have Bantam's catalog filled with hundreds of titles plus take advantage of our unique and exciting bonus book offer. A special offer which gives you the opportunity to purchase a Bantam book for only 50¢. Here's how!

By ordering any five books at the regular price per order, you can also choose any other single book listed (up to a $4.95 value) for just 50¢. Some restrictions do apply, but for further details why not send for Bantam's catalog of titles today!

Just send us your name and address and we will send you a catalog!